How
We
Love

Michael Ryan Webb

In memory of Grandma Janie, who taught me how to read.
In memory of Grandpa Mike, who taught me everything else.
And for Chance, who I love more than I ever thought it was possible
to love someone.

Chapter One | *Adam*

"Be careful with that please," I said to the mover who was clumsily handling a box full of kitchenware as I walked back into the home I was preparing to leave. "I think we're just about done, Mark," I called into the living room.

My husband, Mark, timidly stepped into the foyer, my favorite blue throw blanket in his hands. He looked pitiful. His tall, lanky frame was being swallowed by one of my sweaters. His normally tan skin was pale, having not been exposed to direct sunlight in months. His jet-black hair was unusually long.

"Are you sure?" he asked.

I looked into his sad, brown eyes and wanted

nothing more than to wrap him in my arms and take away his pain. But the last year had taught me that there was nothing I could do. He was fractured, and I was inadequately equipped to fix him and exhausted from trying, among other things. But I couldn't speak the words, so I just nodded.

"Okay," he whispered, barely audible. "You should take these, then." He handed me the blanket, removed the sweater, folded it neatly, and placed it in my hands. Underneath he was wearing a t-shirt that I gave to him on our first Christmas together. I'd think he was wearing it to try to manipulate me into staying if I didn't know that it wasn't in his nature. Without the blanket to hold, he fell into his default action of counting his fingers. I shuddered to think what mental image he was trying to distract from.

"Linda from next door said she'll pick up your medications for you if you let her know when you need them. Make sure you keep taking them," I said to distract us both. "The Millers' boy offered to bring groceries back for you from one of his shifts at the store every week. Just leave some money for him in the garage and he'll leave the food. If you need anything else..." I trailed off. I'd almost told him to call me, but that couldn't be an option.

The tension was graciously broken by one of the movers announcing that they were finished.

"You have to go now," Mark said.

"I have to go now."

"I've never been divorced before. Are we supposed to hug, or like shake hands? Or is this more of a cordial nod and smile situation?" A hint of a smile broke across his unevenly bearded face. There was a tiny glimpse of the humor I'd missed so greatly. If only there had been more of these moments in the last six months than I could count on one hand.

"I think one of us is supposed to enact a crazy scheme that may or may not include posing as an old woman. At least, that's what Robin Williams would have done." I paused, unsure how we were supposed to leave things, then said, "but, we're not actually divorced yet, Mark. I haven't even filed. Who knows -" The smile on his face quickly dissipated.

"Don't give me false hope, Adam. Please."

"No, no, I wasn't trying to do that. I'm sorry."

I saw the moving truck pull away out of the corner of my eye and slowly trudged to the front door.

"I guess this is goodbye, then," I said.

"Just like that?"

I rushed toward him and pulled him into a tight embrace. I haven't the faintest idea how long it lasted. It at once felt both like an eternity and a split-second. He pulled away first, taking me by surprise.

"Take care of yourself, Adam. I-I-I-" he trailed off.

"I know. You too." I hurried out the door, lest I change my mind. I heard Mark close it gently behind me. I threw the blanket and sweatshirt into the backseat of the car that Mark bought me for our 5th wedding anniversary and slid into the driver's seat. I started the car but couldn't bring myself to put it in drive. I looked back up at the house we'd shared for almost a decade and thought back to the day we moved in.

Mark had just won another big case as a defense attorney and the long hours had paid off in the form of a promotion to partner and a bonus check big enough to allow us to finally move out of the crappy apartment we'd lived in since college.

We'd spent over a month looking at houses, determined to find the perfect fit for both of us. When our realtor finally brought us to this moderately sized three-bedroom house in the suburbs, we balked at the idea of it. We hadn't even entertained the thought of children yet. Plus, I was still in graduate school and Mark had just turned 30. The suburbs were no place for us, we insisted. But the second we stepped inside, we'd both dropped our hesitation. Without even seeing the whole thing, it felt like home.

And over the last nine years, we'd made it one. The house bore many signs of our life together. After two years of living there, we were married underneath the large oak tree in the backyard when our original plans fell through. Like love-struck teenagers, we carved our names and the date into the bark of the tree.

A terrible painting that we made together at one of those cheesy classes where you get tipsy on wine and try to paint hung in the foyer. It was covering up the bad drywall repair job we'd done after I insisted on carrying Mark over the threshold after our honeymoon and stumbled into the wall.

There were permanent stains on the carpet in the living room from the many dinners we shared there because the dining room table was invisible underneath the mountain of combined work from Mark's ongoing cases and my research for my doctoral dissertation and later, papers I had to grade.

Yes, the house carried many memories of our life together. But it was the front porch that I found myself unable to look away from. It was there, sitting in front of the bright red door, that I'd proposed to Mark on my 30th birthday. A coworker had jokingly asked me if I'd gotten everything I wanted for my "big day" and it sent me into a tailspin of wondering if I was where I wanted to be at that point in my life. I'd realized by the end of the day that there was only one thing I felt like I needed – to be Mark's husband.

We'd been together for almost ten years by that point. We talked as if we were going to be together forever, but neither of us had ever brought up an actual marriage. Of course, it hadn't really been an option for a lot of our relationship. But it was finally legal, and I'd decided I was ready.

I'd rushed home that afternoon, eager to plan a proposal before Mark got home from work. But when I got there, he'd already organized a surprise party for me. As much as I'd appreciated and enjoyed the party, I was anxious to talk to him about getting married.

While everyone was distracted with cake, I'd snuck upstairs and retrieved a small, stained glass jar out of a box in the back of my closet. It once held a candle we bought on a date to a renaissance fair. That candle had been burning at dinner the night Mark first told me that he loved me. When it ran out, I'd saved the jar as a reminder of that night. Since I didn't have a ring, I'd hoped that a reminder of our love could serve as a token for the proposal.

And it worked. I pulled Mark out to sit on the porch together and thanked him for the party. He poked fun at how surprised I was before asking what I'd wanted to talk about.

"Somebody asked me what I wanted for my

birthday earlier," I said. "And it made me realize how good what we have is. We're creating this beautiful life together that is so much more than I ever dreamed I could have. There's only one thing I really want- you. I mean, forever, for real. I mean – What I'm trying to say is-"

"Of course, I'll marry you," he interrupted, his face glowing with a smile that had always given me butterflies. "What's the jar for?"

"I don't have a ring. But I've saved this since the first night we said, 'I love you', and I wanted to give you something to remind you that I still love you, and I always will."

He loved the gesture. After the party guests dispersed, we sat on the porch planning a wedding and discussing our future. We'd spent many nights since then sitting on that porch, talking about our work and our dreams. It was hard to think about never sitting there across from Mark again. But life doesn't ask for permission to change, and after everything that had been thrown at us over the preceding year, I felt like I had no choice but to go, for both of our sakes.

I pictured us on that porch one last time - happy and in love, full of hope - then slowly pulled away from the curb. I had managed to avoid becoming emotional through most of the process leading up to this day, but in that moment, leaving our home for the last time, I finally broke down.

I calmed myself down when I got to my new apartment for long enough to let the movers in, but then I sat back in the car and sobbed uncontrollably. Had I made a mistake? Was I a monster for giving up on a man I loved so deeply just because things had gotten difficult? I couldn't face the answers to those questions. All I knew was that we'd agreed. He wasn't getting any better; I wasn't helping; and some space would do both of us some good.

When I finally calmed down, I helped the movers unload everything, paid them, and started unpacking. Unsurprisingly, a large majority of my belongings carried memories of Mark. That proved too painful to deal with right away. Instead, I just sat on my bare mattress, surrounded by boxes I was too afraid to open.

You wanted this, I thought to myself. *You needed this. You were suffocating.*

I went for a walk to try to calm my nerves. The university where I taught was only a few blocks away, so I walked to my favorite spot on campus to try to relax. I sat in a courtyard and faced a statue of an open book sitting in the middle of a fountain. The steady water flow was peaceful enough to allow me to clear my mind.

Recommitted to my decision, I went back to my new home and unpacked. I tried to sleep afterward, but the emptiness next to me in the bed was impossible to ignore. Despite all his busy nights working on cases, Mark and I hadn't spent a night apart in nearly 16 years. I tried to watch TV, but since my cable and internet hadn't been installed yet, I only had one fuzzy channel option.

The movie *Hope Floats* was playing, and I found myself wishing that I could trade places with Sandra Bullock's character. At least her husband was an asshole who cheated on her. This would have been so much easier if Mark had cheated on me and given me a reason to hate him.

But the truth was, he hadn't done anything wrong. He'd been struggling with a mental illness that I couldn't understand or help him with, no matter how hard I'd tried, and we had simply grown apart. We just didn't fit anymore. The problem was that I still so desperately wanted us to.

I tossed and turned for several hours until I finally fell asleep out of sheer exhaustion. The next morning, I overslept. For so many years, Mark got up at exactly five o'clock in the morning to get a head-start on his work for the day, and I had grown used to him waking me up later in the morning. Even since he'd been out of work, he'd continued that routine. It never even occurred to me to set an alarm.

Get your shit together, Adam, I thought to myself as I raced to get dressed and get to work. I managed to make it to class right on time but didn't have time to practice my prepared lecture. So, I decided to just wing it. It was an intermediate level creative writing class, so I asked the students to write one page about a big event during their summer from an outsider's perspective and gave them the hour to work on it while I looked over my notes for my next, more advanced class.

Afterward, as I pored over their work and made notes of what areas to focus on throughout the semester for each student, I came across a longer than required entry. The student, Lauren, detailed her tumultuous relationship drama with her on-again, off-again boyfriend. He'd claimed to be completely committed to her at the beginning of the year, "for real this time."

So, at the end of the spring semester, she'd transferred here and moved across the country to be with him, only to have him grow distant and eventually break up with her, leaving her to find a new place to live and get through at least the next semester in a new place where she knew only him. Throughout, she took the viewpoint of a concerned friend watching herself make bad decisions, but never tried to paint herself as a victim.

I marveled at her resilience. How weak was I that I was falling apart in a new setting of my own design, while this young woman was handling being left in the lurch like a champ? What was I doing moping around? The whole point of this separation was so that I could have the space I felt like I needed. I spent so long feeling like a jerk for wanting it before I decided I really did need it. So why did it still feel terrible now that I had it?

I reminded myself that this was supposed to be better and decided to really try harder to enjoy my newfound freedom and be happy. I made plans with a couple of colleagues to go out for drinks that evening and managed to get through the rest of my day without letting myself get down again.

At the end of the day, the thought of waiting around my apartment seemed like asking for trouble, so I headed over to the bar early. Sofia's place, named after the owner, was popular with teachers because it was the only bar in town that had a strict 25 and up policy. Sofia herself still tended the bar, and she had no patience for the drunk shenanigans of college students.

I scooted into a booth in the back and ordered dinner and a drink to pass the time. By the time my colleagues, Amy and Wes, arrived, I was on my fourth rum and Coke. Amy, a tiny ball of energy with black hair and piercing green eyes, was a recent doctorate graduate specializing in Victorian Gothic fiction. We'd bonded over a shared sense of humor and our husbands got along well, so we'd spent plenty of time together over the years.

Wes was still a graduate student but had attached himself to me upon learning that I was an openly gay professor. As a gay man himself, I suppose he thought we'd have plenty in common. We didn't. I'd only really invited him along because he had a way of easily filling any silence or gaps in conversation, and I thought it would be easy to avoid talking about my separation with him around.

Ironically, Wes had just gone through a break up himself and hearing him process it by speaking about it made me feel like I should try it too. When Amy finally asked me if anything new happened with me over the summer, I tossed back my drink and said, "I left Mark."

Their reactions immediately made me regret my words. Amy was notoriously non-interested in other people's drama, but her mouth dropped open and her eyes darted back and forth between me and Wes, who choked on his drink.

"What are you talking about? What happened?" Amy asked.

"There's officially no hope for me now," Wes lamented.

"Shut up," she said, smacking his arm. "When did this happen?"

"Yesterday," I whispered.

"Oh my god. Are you okay?" she asked.

"Yesterday? Sweetie what are you doing out? You should be at home eating ice cream in sweats and trolling Grindr while you watch bad TV," he opined.

"Wes," Amy said through gritted teeth, "Could you get us some more drinks?"

"But I'm gonna miss the drama," he whined.

I saw Amy try to discreetly stomp on his foot under the table and wanted out of the conversation.

"I'll do it," I said. "I'll be right back."

I trudged up to the bar and found Sofia restocking. She was an older woman who'd come to America from Mexico as a young girl. She was now probably in her late 60s, but she still had the fire of a 20-something. She had a big, hearty laugh that could fill the entire bar, and most of the wrinkles on her face appeared to be smile lines. I hadn't been much of a drinker in the last decade, but when I did I always enjoyed going to her place and talking with her.

"What'll it be, Blue-Eyes?" she asked in a deep southern drawl that reminded me of my small Texan hometown.

"Another round for me and the gang, ma'am. Make mine a double, please."

She made the drinks with all the flair you'd expect of someone with her experience, handed them over, watched me chug mine, and laughed as she poured me another.

"I hope that sexy husband of yours is on his way to get you. Driving just went out the window for you, young man," she quipped, holding her hand out for my keys.

"Well, he's not really my husband anymore... So that'd be a surprise," I said, handing her my keys. I hadn't meant to say that, but I'd also lost track of how many drinks I'd had by then.

"*Lo siento, Mijo.*" She grabbed two glasses and filled them up. "To fresh starts," she said, holding up one of the glasses. I tapped my glass against hers and we drank.

"Are you supposed to be drinking while you bartend?"

"Honey, I'm a grown-ass woman and this here is my bar. I do what I want," she said with a wink. "Now go on back to your friends. The *gringo* looks like he's about ready to explode waiting for you to come back"

I thanked her and made my way back to my seat. Amy and Wes were bickering when I reached them. They quickly shushed each other and stared at me expectantly as I sat back down.

"Well, what happened?" Wes finally asked, practically shouting.

I took a long drink and a deep breath before finally saying, "It just wasn't working. I don't know. Maybe it can still work out. Maybe this separation will give us both time to get to a place where we're better for each other. But for now, I just need space."

"Oh, Adam. I'm so sorry," Amy said. Her phone buzzed. "Oh, great. It's Jason. He tried to change the oil in his car without me and can't figure out what to do. Mind if I go call him?"

"Actually, I better get going anyway," I lied, not wanting to think about the fact that she still had a happy marriage. "Still have a lot of unpacking to do."

"Okay, well you call me if you need anything," she said. "Wes, I feel like I'm going to regret asking, but can you please make sure he gets home safely?"

"Obviously." He rolled his eyes.

I swallowed what was left of my drink and slowly fumbled my way back out of the booth. In the time I'd been back from the bar, those drinks had hit me pretty hard. Wes helped me out to his car and spoke dramatically about how hard single life was as he drove me back to my apartment. I couldn't keep up with his speech. I just nodded and leaned against the window.

After what felt like hours, we finally arrived at my apartment. I insisted I could get upstairs by myself but stumbled by the third step. Wes rushed to steady me and helped me up the stairs.

"You wanna come in for another drink?" I asked, my words already slurring as I struggled to open the door.

"I'm like 1000% sure you've already had enough. Here, sit down. I'll get you some water," he said, guiding me to the couch.

I slowly drank some of the water he brought me, but still spilled some on both of us.

"Shit, I'll be right back. Make yourself at home, if you can find anything," I said, stumbling away. I clumsily changed my clothes and grabbed a towel and an extra t-shirt for Wes.

But when I got back to the living room, he was completely naked, dropping his clothes into the dryer.

"What the hell are you doing?" I shouted.

"When I stood up, the water ran down my pants, duh. I wasn't gonna sit around wet."

"Well, here! Cover up," I shouted, throwing the towel and shirt to him and trying not to look below his neckline. "I'll go grab some sweatpants or something."

Suddenly feeling very sober, I quickly

rummaged through boxes and found a pair of Mark's pajamas that I had taken by mistake. I dropped to the floor and started crying.

"Do you want me to put on pants or not?" Wes called, coming into the room. "Oh, hey, what's wrong?"

"The first pants I found are Mark's," I sobbed.

"Oh, no, Adam. Don't cry, come here." He dropped to the floor next to me and wrapped his arms around me. He hugged me while I cried until it was out of my system.

When I had finally calmed down, I realized that for the first time in almost a year, someone was taking care of me. I wasn't trying to take care of him or anticipate his needs. *He* was there for *me.* That realization coupled with the overindulgence from the evening led me to do something so enormously stupid that I may never live down the embarrassment.

I looked up at him, he smiled, and I kissed him. I fully expected him to punch me in the face, but he surprised me by kissing me back. I was very briefly caught up in an adrenaline rush. Then he spoke.

"God, this is perfect. We both needed to get laid."

Suddenly I remembered the multitude of reasons why Wes was not someone I would normally consider doing this with. It wasn't that he wasn't attractive. He was, in a very basic-handsome-young-white-man way. His blonde hair was styled in a trendy cut and he was in good physical shape. He was generally nice to look at. But he was also one of the most irritating people I'd ever met. He was self-centered beyond reason, loud, and careless. Of course, by the next morning, I'd think of myself as a much worse person than that.

Plus, I had literally been separated from my husband for one day. It was much too soon. But I was very drunk, and he was young and attractive, grating personality be damned. I grabbed him and kissed him again.

"Oh my god. I've always secretly thought you were so hot," he said, taking a breath. "Not like... hot-hot, but like...teacher-hot."

"Hey, do me a favor if we're gonna do this? Don't talk."

The rest was a blur of more drinks and things that I'd only done with Mark for the last two decades. I almost sobered up when I had to explain to Wes that my last name was only Diaz by marriage because he asked me to, "say something sexy in Spanish," but a couple of shots of whiskey got me right back into it. When it was over, I felt both relieved and guilty. I was too far gone to process the guilt, so I decided to avoid trying to until the next day.

"Okay, I take it back. You are definitely more than teacher-hot," Wes said, heading for the living room.

"Thanks, I guess. Where are you going?"

"Gotta get my clothes so I can get out of here," he called back. When he re-entered the bedroom, putting his clothes on, he continued, "If I go home now, this stays a 'friends with benefits' thing. If I spend the night, it's gonna be weird in the morning."

"Oh, yeah, totally," I said, pretending to understand the now apparently much more complicated rules of sex and dating.

"So, I'll see you at school tomorrow, then. Great

work, by the way," he said, extending his hand for a high-five.

I awkwardly pressed my hand against his, and then he was gone. When I heard his car pull away downstairs and was sure he was gone, I rolled over and shouted into my pillow, one searing thought repeating in my head: *What the hell have I done?*

Chapter Two | *Mark*

*1,2,3,4,5,6,7,8,9,10,1,2,3,4,5,6,7,8,9,10,1,2,3,4,5
,6,7,8,9,10*

I counted my fingers over and over, trying to calm myself down. The alternative was to let in the bad thoughts that I so terribly wanted to get out of my mind. I stopped counting to try to peak out the window to see if Adam had pulled away from the house yet and was immediately greeted with the mental image of myself falling on the sidewalk and a rock stabbing me in the eye. Back to counting.

*1,2,3,4,5,6,7,8,9,10,1,2,3,4,5,6,7,8,9,10,1,2,3,4,5
,6,7,8,9,10*

I slowly made my way through the house to the cabinet where my medications were stored. I carefully opened the door, being sure to keep my face away from the corners. But my mind was overcome with the image of the corner of the door hitting me in the eye and leaving splinters embedded. I dropped to the cold, tile floor and rubbed my eye seven times, assuring myself that it was fine. My hands were shaking too much to count my fingers, so I resorted to counting the stripes on the shower curtain to bring myself back to reality.

1,2,3,4,5,6,7,8,1,2,3,4,5,6,7,8,1,2,3,4,5,6,7,8,1,2, 3,4,5,6,7,8

When I could finally bear to face the cabinet again, I quickly snatched my medications and darted out of the room. As I hurried into the family room past the sofa, my foot brushed the tassel of a throw blanket hanging from the side, and my mind was filled with images of snakes surrounding me and biting at my feet. I scurried into a nearby recliner and scratched at my foot, trying to convince myself that the images in my head weren't real.

After I calmed down, I tried to come up with something to distract myself. I considered knitting, an old hobby I hadn't tried in a while, and instantly pictured myself slipping and shoving one of the needles into my eye. Back to the rubbing.

1,2,3,4,5,6,7

I walked carefully upstairs to retrieve my phone and back to the recliner, counting my steps along the way to keep my mind occupied.

1,2,3,4,5,6,7,8,9,10,11,12,13,14,15,16,17,18,19, 20,21,22....

I almost dialed Adam's number, like a reflex. I reminded myself that that was no longer an option and scrolled through my contacts for other ideas. Work and my marriage had consumed so much of my life in the last several years that I hadn't committed much time to making friends.

Our neighbors were friendly enough, but like most small communities, tended to err on the side of gossip. There was a couple we had become friends with, Amy and Jason. But that friendship was born of Amy and Adam working together, so I wasn't sure I should reach out to them.

I came to the number of Kate, an old friend from law school and decided to call and catch up with her, hoping a conversation would distract me long enough for my medication to kick in. I pushed the call button and listened to the ringing.

You know she never actually liked you, the voice in my head blared. *She only pretended to be your friend because you wouldn't stop talking to her in class.*

"Shut up. Shut up. Shut up. Shut up. Shut up," I whispered to myself.

"Hi. You've reached the voicemail of Kate Sanchez. If this is related to a legal matter, please call my office. If this is a personal call, please leave a message and I will get back to you as promptly as possible. Thank you," the machine chirped.

I told you, the voice gloated. *You could dial every number on that phone and no one is going to pick up because no one wants to talk to you. You're a burden. You always have been. And now that you ruined your career and your marriage, no one needs to pretend otherwise anymore.*

I reminded myself that the voice was *my* voice – that I could get control of it back if I tried hard enough. I made my way to the kitchen, gathered supplies to make cookies, and turned on the small TV in the corner of the room. Baking and *Judge Judy* reruns were two of my favorite pastimes. Surely both at the same time would ease my mind long enough for my medication to calm me down.

My father had always loved to cook. We very seldom ate out when I was a child for the simple reason that he loved to be in the kitchen. Some of my clearest, fondest memories of him are ones where he let me help him with whatever he was cooking. I never quite picked up his skills, but I was much better at baking. The precision required for it clicked better in my mind, I suppose, so I did that to feel close to him after he died. Still, I kept a stack of his old recipes in my own recipe box, hoping someday I'd work up the nerve to try them myself.

I began mixing ingredients, weighing each meticulously, and carefully combining them, finally focused enough on something to block out any disturbing mental images. I slid the prepared cookie dough into the oven just in time.

The weighted haze of the medication set in and I had to sit down. I hated the way it made me feel, like I was sedated and just drifting through life. But it was better than the alternative.

I turned my attention to the TV and tried to engage myself in a game I liked to play to try to wake myself up a bit. I watched the ridiculous guests on *Judge Judy* try to argue their sides and imagined what kind of case I would build if I were hired to represent either of them. The show went to a commercial break and I leaned my head back and closed my eyes. I almost dozed off, but a commercial caught my attention.

It advertised a web therapy site and featured a few glowing reviews of the "licensed local professionals." Not long before, I would have laughed at the idea of something like that. But I had pretty much hit rock bottom and saw nothing else to lose from giving it a shot.

I waited until the cookies were finished and set them out to cool while I retreated to my office. I sat in the oversized chair that Adam bought me for our first wedding anniversary because he thought sitting in my old one felt, "like sitting in something Wednesday

Addams designed to torture regular people."

I sunk down into the chair and picked up a nearby photo of Adam. He had been smiling at me as I took the picture. Behind his dark brown hair, the sunset was creating a halo effect. His blue eyes were shining as bright as ever. That picture was at one time a source of comfort, but it made me feel sad with him gone.

I turned the photo down and allowed myself to get lost in memories of our life together. I thought back to the big moments – the first time we met, the first night we spent in the house, the proposal, the wedding – each one now just an echo of a love that had eroded under pressure, possibly beyond repair.

I signed up for the website and was surprised to find that I could speak with a therapist in just a few minutes. While I waited, I returned to my thoughts. I tried to think of good times, happy memories that would remind me that I had something to fight for.

I thought about the night I first said, "I love you," to Adam. I hadn't planned it. We'd gone hiking earlier in the day and I kept looking over at him as he talked to me and felt completely and totally enamored with the way his eyes seemed to shine brighter than the golden sun beaming down on us.

That night, we picked up tacos from his favorite truck, and I felt giddy watching how happily he talked to the people there and remembered exactly what I liked. We went back to his place and had just started eating when a storm rolled in and knocked the power out. He didn't have a flashlight, but he did have a candle we'd bought the week before at a renaissance fair.

He lit the candle, pulled me up, and started to lead me in dancing. When I said we needed music, he started humming one of my favorite songs. I laid my head on his shoulder and sighed, "I love you." He said it back, his beautiful eyes radiating in the candlelight; and everything else grew from that moment.

I got emotional and lost control. My mind was flooded with images of Adam getting into a car accident on his way to his new apartment.

And it would be all your fault, the voice in my head chimed in.

1,2,3,4,5,6,7,8,9,10,1,2,3,4,5,6,7,8,9,10....

I counted my fingers and took deep breaths. My

heart was pounding so hard I could feel it in my ear drums. I felt like I might pass out. Then the computer chimed, and I snapped out of it.

"Good afternoon, Mr. Diaz," a chipper voice said through the speakers.

I looked up to find a woman smiling at me on the screen. She was young, probably in her mid-twenties. She appeared very well put-together. Her suit was neatly pressed, and her long brown hair was pulled into a tight bun. But her smile was warm and her eyes kind.

"Um, hello," I muttered.

"Hi. My name is Dr. Rodriguez. You can call me Hannah if you'd like. Whatever you're most comfortable with."

"Thanks," I said, barely audible. I was suddenly very nervous. Had I jumped into this prematurely? Was I ready for this stranger to ask me personal questions?

No turning back now, I thought to myself.

"Why don't you start by telling me a little about yourself?" she asked. "Let's start with age, occupation, marital status, the basics."

Marital status? Ouch. Ditto occupation.

"Okay-so-I-um- I'm 39 years old," I started shakily. "I-um- technically am unemployed right now, but I normally am a defense attorney. And, well, as of a couple of hours ago, I am separated from my husband."

"I'm sorry to hear that. Is that what prompted you to contact us today?"

"Yes and no – sort of."

"Let's start with the yes," she said, smiling sympathetically. "How are you feeling about the separation? I take it this wasn't your decision?"

"Not exactly. I mean, I agreed that he should go, if he wanted; and when it became clear that he really did want to, I didn't try to stop him."

"Why not?"

"It didn't seem like I had a right to argue. He didn't want to be with me anymore, and I couldn't really blame him." I felt defensive but did my best to quell that feeling.

"I'm guessing that brings us to the "no" part of why you came to us," she said. "Can you tell me why you felt that way?"

"I suppose I felt like I'd become something of a burden to him," I said after a long pause. "I-um-I have been struggling with OCD and major depression for the last year or so."

"I see. Have you been seeing anyone for treatment and medication before today?"

"Well, I was. I haven't in a while," I admitted. "For the past few months, I haven't really been able to leave my home. I just-" I paused. I could hear my own voice wavering. "I don't even feel safe here. The thought of setting foot in the real world where I have no control over anything is too terrifying."

"I understand," she said. She paused for a moment and smiled. "I have some good news for you, Mr. Diaz. We can fix this. I absolutely believe that. OCD is a nasty beast, but it is manageable. We need to speak more in depth of course, and probably change your medication up a bit, but I believe we can get you back on your feet. I can't promise that all your symptoms will disappear completely, or that all the problems that this disease has caused for you will suddenly repair themselves. But I can promise to be here for you, and help you learn to take back control of your life. Can you trust me to help you?"

I had been to a few different psychiatrists over the preceding year and hadn't gotten anywhere with any of them. To say that I was hesitant to trust another one would be a massive understatement. But she seemed sincerely interested in helping and I was in no position to turn that down. So, I finally said, "Yes, I think so."

"Great," she said, beaming. "Then I'd like to ask you some more questions now, if that's okay."

"Of course."

"Have you been taking your medication regularly?" she asked.

"I have, and it helps for a bit; but it also makes me feel too heavily sedated to function much."

"Okay. Well, we definitely have options on that front. I'm going to write you a prescription for something new that hopefully won't give you that drowsy feeling. We'll try that for a couple of weeks and see where that gets us. In the meantime, I'd like to try to unpack what's happening to you and what may have triggered it in this later stage of your life as opposed to early adulthood. You said you've only been experiencing these symptoms for about a year. Did anything traumatic happen around the time that your symptoms started? Perhaps marital issues?"

I thought back and tried to discern when the symptoms started. "I suppose it started shortly after my dad died. We were also trying to adopt at the time and it fell through. My symptoms started out innocently enough. I suddenly became very particular about where things went, but plenty of people are particular. So, I didn't think anything of it."

I took a shallow breath and continued, "Then the aversion to germs kicked in. A client sneezed on my desk – something that I'm sure had happened at least once before. But I couldn't stop obsessing over it. I felt like my skin was on fire. I tried to wipe down the area in front of where she'd been sitting, and that helped for a few minutes, but then I just kept thinking that it was still dirty. As the day went on I became convinced that there was some type of airborne disease in my office and that it would kill me. By the time the day was over

I had scrubbed everything on the desk and ultimately ordered a new one and told my assistant I would be working from home until it arrived. Everything went downhill from there."

Her smile had faded slightly, and she looked concerned as she asked, "You say your father passed recently? Were the two of you close?"

I wanted to give an honest answer, so I tried to seriously consider what our relationship had been like.

The answer is "no", moron, the voice in my head interrupted. *You're not close with anyone because no one would ever* want *to be close to you.*

Then my mind fixated on an image of my father, lying lifeless in his bed. I desperately began counting my fingers.

1,2,3,4,5,6,7,8,9,10,1,2,3,4,5,6,7,8,9,10,1,2,3,4,5 ,6,7,8,9,10...

"Mr. Diaz? Mr. Diaz," I heard Dr. Rodriguez calling. "I lost you for a minute there. Are you okay?" she asked as I finally came back to reality.

"I'm sorry. I just-"

"You were having a compulsion," she said. I

nodded weakly and she continued, "May I ask if it was triggered by something? Was there an obsessive thought? It's okay if you aren't ready to talk about it."

1,2,3,4,5,6,7,8,9,10,1,2,3,4,5,6,7,8,9,10,1,2,3,4,5 ,6,7,8,9,10

I continued counting while I explained. "When my dad died. I was the one who found his body. Sometimes the image of him lying there, not moving, not breathing -" I paused to compose myself. "It haunts me. It's unshakable. With the other obsessions, there's something I can do to manage them. But this one – this one eats at me like a living nightmare until my brain decides it's done torturing me."

"I'm so sorry. I can only imagine how traumatic that must be. I asked before if you had a good relationship with your father and that seemed to trigger the mental image. Is that because the relationship was strained?" she asked.

"Not at all," I answered, finally sure of my answer. "He was sort of my hero. My mom was never really around so it was just us. He always made sure I had everything I needed, even if it meant he had to do without something. He supported me unconditionally."

"So now that he's gone, do you perhaps feel an absence of sorts?" she asked.

"I guess I do," I said, the weight of the answer hitting me like a freight train. "I guess without him I feel like there's this fundamental piece of me missing – like I have no idea who I am or where I belong anymore. It feels like... like I lost a leg, and now I have to learn how to walk again, only there's no prosthetic to catch me. So, no matter how hard I try, I just keep falling."

That's not because you lost your dad, it's because you're a worthless nobody, the voice in my head chimed in. I gritted my teeth, gripped the arms of my chair tightly, and ignored it.

"I imagine the dissolution of your marriage has only compounded that feeling," Dr. Rodriguez said.

"Of course. Now I'm completely alone and I have no idea where to even start picking up the pieces of my life."

"Well, you've already started," she said, smiling. "You've acknowledged that you need help and you've reached out. Those are not things to take lightly. Treating mental illness is all about baby steps, and you've started down the road to healing. You should be very proud of that."

I nodded weakly, unsure I agreed with her, but willing to buy into it for the time being.

"Do you have a support system outside of your husband? Are there any friends or other family members you can turn to when you can't handle things alone?" she asked.

"Not really," I admitted. "I suppose that's part of the problem. Most of my social circle was composed of work colleagues. The rest are friends I shared with Adam and I'm not sure how to talk to them about our separation."

"That's understandable," she said. "In that case, what I would like for you to do before our next session, assuming you decide to continue working with me – and I hope you do – is reach out to someone. It can be anyone who you trust. Try to open up to them. Even if you can't talk to them about these issues right off the bat, at least try to open the door. I believe therapy will help, but I also believe that a strong support system in your daily life is vital. Can you do that for me?"

"I can try."

Good luck, dumbass. No one wants to hear from you, remember? The voice in my head continued to mock me.

"Good," Dr. Rodriguez said. "Well I think that's about all we have time for today, but I'd like to schedule an appointment with you for this time next week if that's okay." I nodded in agreement and she continued, "Great. In the meantime, I'll send this new prescription over to your local pharmacy for you. I'd like for you to try keeping a log of any particularly strong obsessions or compulsions, what you were doing when they started, and how you managed them. Email that to me the night before your next appointment so that I can get a better picture of exactly what you're dealing with."

"I will. Thank you."

"Thank you for reaching out, Mark. I truly believe you are going to be okay. Have a nice week," she said, warmly.

I slouched back into my chair and wondered what to do with myself for the next week. I started browsing news online to keep my mind occupied, but the temptation to check in on Adam's social media profiles was too strong. I moved away from the computer and was just about to start cleaning the already spotless living room when my phone went off.

New Message from Kate Sanchez, it read.

Maybe I'm not so alone after all, I thought.

Chapter Three | *Adam*

The next day at work, I quarantined myself to my office and classrooms all day so that I wouldn't risk running into Wes. That just gave me ample time between my classes to feel guilty about the previous night.

One day, I thought. *You couldn't make it one day on your own without royally fucking up.*

During a long break between classes, I tried to occupy myself by cleaning out my office. Big mistake, of course. I quickly found myself surrounded by mementos of my life with Mark. There was a picture of us on our honeymoon hanging next to my diplomas. A stuffed animal he won for me on a date to a carnival sat on top of one of my filing cabinets. Sweet little notes he had written and hidden around for me to find kept popping up.

I finally gave up and decided to take a walk. I ended up at the book fountain and tried to relax. I closed my eyes, took a deep breath, and tried to focus on the sound of the running water. It must have been working because I didn't hear anyone approach before I was being tapped on the shoulder.

"Dr. Diaz... Dr. Diaz?" a familiar voice asked.

I opened my eyes to find Dr. Ana Lewis, the head of my department. She was a very tall woman, and the sun glaring behind her head coupled with the way her dark skin made it hard to read her expression in the shadows gave her an intimidating appearance. But Ana was one of the kindest people I'd ever known.

"Oh, I'm so sorry Dr. Lewis. I was, um, meditating."

"No need to apologize, Diaz. I hear you've got a lot going on," she said, sitting next to me.

"You do?"

"Mr. Harris was perhaps not the best choice of confidant if you hoped to keep it a secret," she said with a smirk.

I'm gonna fucking strangle Wes, I thought.

"I suppose you're right. I'm sorry I was running late this morning. I promise it will not happen again. It was-" I started to explain, flustered, but she cut me off.

"Again, no need," she said, smiling. "I actually intended to speak with you about something else. I had a rather interesting conversation with Dr. Andrews this morning. It seems he has been offered a position at another university and has opted to take it. Why he waited until the semester was already in session to inform me of this, I don't know. However, as I'm sure you know, he leaves behind several senior level courses that I need someone I can trust to take over. You were my first thought."

"Oh, wow, thank you, Dr. Lewis. I'm honored, truly. But, in the wake of the personal information you were given by We- Mr. Harris, are you sure that's a good idea?" I asked.

"I imagine only you can answer that," she said matter-of-factly. "I'll leave you to think it over. However, I will need an answer by the end of the day so that I can assess my other options if necessary."

"Of course. I will get back to you as quickly as

possible. Thank you again."

"Thank me when you say yes, Diaz," she said, leaving me behind with a quick pat on the knee.

"Oh, Dr. Lewis. It's – it's King now, I suppose. At least, it will be soon"

"Dr. King, then," she said with a gentle smile. And then she was off. I watched her walk back inside, each step self-assured and purposeful. I hoped I could get it together and be half that composed soon.

I sat and listened to the fountain until I had to go to my next class. It was the same intermediate creative writing class as the day before. After reading through their first assignments, I knew I had my work cut out for me.

As the students filed in, I noticed a few new faces. In a class that had been full the day before, I knew that meant I had already scared a few of them off. *Better now than after wasting all of our time,* I thought. At least, I thought that until I realized that Lauren, the girl who's paper I had been touched by the day before, was one of the missing students.

I pulled an updated class roster and found that

Lauren Carter was still enrolled. I quickly sent her an e-mail asking if everything was okay, then proceeded with class. I had each student stand and talk to the class about why they'd decided to take the class and what they hoped to get from it. The answers ranged from pointless to stupid to actually intriguing. We discussed questions they had over the previous day's assignment and looked over a few examples together. Then I sent them off with a writing assignment.

When everyone was gone, I checked my email and found one from Lauren explaining that she'd had an emergency but would make up any missed work the next day.

I couldn't explain why, but I felt a sense of responsibility for this girl. Maybe it was because she so clearly felt alone here. Maybe it was because I now understood that feeling all too well. In any case, I couldn't help but worry about her as I made my way back to my office. I was so concerned, in fact, that I was completely unaware of Wes coming down the hall in my direction until he was turning into my office behind me and shutting the door.

"Hey, so I was thinking about last night," he began before I had a chance to speak. "And I think we should make it, like, a regular thing. Like, this semester is gonna be *really* stressful for me, and probably for you too. So, like, why waste time hunting for fun when you can shop local?"

He was clearly trying to be flirty, but my sober brain had a very different reaction to it than my drunk brain did. Sober, I was unwaveringly aware of all of the reasons why I only spent time with Wes when Amy was around to be a buffer.

"You know what, can we talk about this later? I actually have this really important meeting with Dr. Lewis to get to." I was lying. I hadn't really even had a chance to give Ana's proposal much thought. But I was not prepared to deal with this mess yet.

"Oh, are you taking over that troll Dr. Andrews's classes? Because that's even more reason we should definitely keeping hooking up," he said, not missing a beat.

"Ye-um-I, I gotta go," I said, quickly sliding between him and the door. *Put that on the list of reasons* not *to take on the extra classes,* I thought.

I walked toward Dr. Lewis's office in case he was watching, then cut for Amy's office at the last minute. She wasn't in there, so I sent her a text message: "Can I hide in your office?"

"Only if you want me to come kill you. Hall C. Now," she replied.

So much for wondering if she knows, I thought.

I begrudgingly made my way to Study Hall C, a room reserved for freshman English students to study that was never used because the professors who taught the lowest level classes always failed to mention it. It mostly ended up being used for professors who wanted a place to hide that wasn't their offices.

I found Amy angrily tilting a Nintendo 3DS as if it was going to help whatever she was doing. "No, no, no, no, NO, come on! Fucking blue shell," she yelled, slamming the game down.

"Bad time?" I asked, half hoping she'd say yes.

"Well, a better time would have been before you fucked Loud Mouth Lou, but I guess that bird already kamikazed out of the nest, didn't it," she said. She sounded angry, but the look on her face told me she was at least half joking.

"So, you heard about that, huh?" I asked, feigning ignorance.

"Are you kidding? I heard about it in *excruciating* detail. You're lucky I didn't throw up the $8 breakfast burrito I was eating because I would definitely have billed you," she said, smacking my arm. "What the fuck could you possibly have been thinking, Adam?"

"I *wasn't.* That's the problem," I said, laying my head on the table.

"You haven't even filed divorce papers yet. Have you?"

"No. I know, I'm a monster."

"Okay, now hold on. You obviously have the intention of doing so, and you guys are definitely done right?"

"Well, that's the idea," I said, picking my head slightly up off the table and slamming it back down. "I don't know, Amy. I mean, I feel awful, but at the same time – we agreed to a divorce right? So part of me thinks I didn't technically do anything wrong, but another part of me feels like if I have to rely on a technicality then I definitely *did* do something wrong. And in either case this was exactly the very last thing I needed right now."

"Well, do you want to know what I think you need to do now?"

"Why do I feel like you're gonna say, 'suck it up, buttercup'?" I asked, bracing myself for her favorite catchphrase.

"Because you need to suck it up, buttercup," she said, not even a hint of irony in her voice. "You fucked up. So what? We all make mistakes. Twice last week, Jason only picked up one of our two kids from daycare. *Twice.* Shit happens. And even though this mistake makes me want to do the world's biggest spit-take, what's done is done. You and Mark are not together right now and you and Wes are both adults. Sort of. I mean, we both know Wes behaves like a 17-year old, but he is technically a grown man. So, do I think you should do it again? Dear God, no. But I also wouldn't say you did anything wrong. Maybe just cut back on the drinking for a while, or at least get better at making drunk decisions."

I still felt guilty, but she made some decent points. Surely I would have moved on to someone else eventually. Plus, I was certain that had I not been the drunkest I'd ever been in my life, Wes would never have ended up back at my apartment.

"Thanks, Amy. I appreciate that."

"Anytime, young Padawan," she said, patting my head gently. "Now go forth and be single. I gotta go call Jason and make sure he remembers to feed the kids tonight while I go to some bullshit Homeowners Association meeting."

"Amy, is Jason okay?"

"Of course he is, dude. He's just an idiot like every other man," she said with a wink, heading for the door. She turned back right before she exited. "Oh, and you should definitely take Andrews' classes. Guy was a hack anyway. You'll do great."

"Is *anything* a secret around here?" I yelled after her.

"Not a chance, babe. Love you, bye," she called

from the hallway.

I laid my head back down on the table and thought of all of the times Amy and I had teased our husbands together when we'd go out for dinner or to each other's houses. I hadn't until that moment considered all of the little things that giving up my marriage meant I'd be giving up along with it.

No more feeling sorry for myself, I thought. *Time to suck it up.*

I had a few minutes before my next class, so I stopped by Dr. Lewis's office.

"If it still stands, I'd like to take you up on your offer."

"Wonderful," she said, smiling. "I have three courses for you. Fortunately the timing of them already worked out so that they don't conflict with your current schedule."

She pulled a large box filled with books and paperwork onto her desk.

"This is everything Dr. Andrews had prepared for them," she said. "You're welcomed to change anything you feel is appropriate. However, since many of your new students will have already purchased the textbooks, I would recommend you not change those. If you do, be sure to give them plenty of time to make exchanges."

"Of course," I said, my voice cracking.

I don't know what I expected, but this was not it. This single box contained almost twice the material I had for the classes I was already set to teach. I immediately began praying that I was not in over my head.

"Well, I better get to it," I said, nervously. "Need to make sure I'm ready for tomorrow."

"I'd expect no less," Dr. Lewis said. "I trust we'll see great things come out of the students, and yourself."

"Thank you again, Dr. Lewis."

I headed to my last class of the day and spent most of the following half hour trying not to worry about everything in that box. I ended class early under the guise of giving the students extra reading time.

I hauled the box home with me and spread all of the material out on the dining table, trying to decide where to start. I was halfway through sorting everything when I realized it looked just like the dining table covered in work I'd shared with Mark when I was in grad school. I slammed everything back into the box and moved into my bedroom, but was quickly distracted by thoughts of the night before.

I tried to make myself focus, but my thoughts alternated between the night I'd spent with Wes and the many evenings I'd spent bouncing ideas around with Mark about my lesson plans and his ongoing cases. Five minutes later I was sitting in my car at the stop sign nearest my former home. Part of me wanted to run inside and scoop him up into my arms and apologize for being such a colossal asshole. But a louder, more persistent voice in my head was telling me that there was a good reason I'd left.

Of course, that voice had nothing to offer in the way of assuaging my guilt for my drunken tryst the night before. *Even if he forgave me for leaving, he'd never forgive me for that,* I thought. But I knew that wasn't true. Mark was always the more selfless and empathetic half of our relationship.

If I was completely honest with myself, I knew that I had been a bad husband over the last year. I loved him as much as I was humanly capable of doing. But for some reason my instinct had been not to stand by him and work through our issues, but to run as fast as I could. I fought that instinct as long as I could, yet I found myself looking in on what used to be my life – a life I'd blown up because I had the emotional maturity of a goldfish.

I started to drive forward, my mind made up to knock on the door and beg Mark to take me back. But I had been so focused on my own thoughts that I'd again forgotten to take in what was happening around me. I had pulled out in front of a small truck that hadn't had a stop sign and as such hadn't slowed. Luckily the woman driving was quick-footed and slammed on her brakes just in time to stop within inches of my door.

I quickly pulled over at the beginning of the block, fully expecting her to come up and give me the dressing down I deserved. But she just drove off. I closed my eyes and sobbed, every emotion I'd been forcing down all day erupting at once. My chest tightened and I could barely breathe.

I couldn't for the life of me fathom what was wrong with me that I had made such utterly shit-poor choices. I cried for every single stupid thing I'd done in the past 48 hours. But more than anything else, I cried because I had just come to the realization that I didn't deserve Mark anymore, and maybe I never did.

I turned the radio to an innocuous talk show to try to drown out my thoughts. I opened my eyes and tried to take deep breaths. I was only three houses down from Mark's, and as I tried to steady myself, I could have sworn that I saw the blinds in one of the bedroom windows draw back slightly.

I panicked and sped away back toward the university. I rushed up to my office and sat underneath my desk, hoping and praying that everyone had gone for the day. But karma works fast and within minutes, I heard someone knock on and then open the door. I quickly wiped my eyes and stood up, trying my best to pretend I was just picking up something I'd dropped.

Wes pushed his way in and casually sat down on the corner of my desk as if it were something he did regularly – it wasn't. He had a look in his eyes and a smirk on his face that were very clearly trouble. I needed to nip whatever this was in the bud. I stepped back as far away from him as I could in the small room before I began speaking.

"Look, Wes, we should talk about last night," I started.

"Why talk when we could do much more fun things with our mouths," he said, in what I can only assume was supposed to be a "sexy" voice, but sounded far from it.

"See, that's exactly the problem. I can't be your, um, whatever it is you think you want me to be. What happened between us was a fluke. It shouldn't have happened the first time, and there definitely cannot be a second time."

"So, what? You got all the use out of me that you wanted and now I'm just yesterday's plaything like your husband?" He demanded, his voice rising sharply.

"Whoa, watch it," I snapped. "We were drunk, we made a mistake. It's over. There's no reason we can't just go back to having a normal professional relationship. In fact, there's no other option. And it was not about using you. If anything you used me. I was hammered and upset, and you were looking for the first bed you could jump into."

"How did I not realize until now that you're such a stupid bitch?" he shot back, stomping toward the door.

"Yeah, well you've got the stupid part right because I always knew you were an irritating child and I was still dumb enough to sleep with you," I retorted.

Well, it was ugly, but at least it's over, I thought as the door slammed. I'd planned to try to work out my lesson plans once I calmed down, but I decided I'd had more than enough excitement for one day. I emailed my new students and let them know we'd be skipping the next day's classes in order to accommodate the instructor change, and hurried to my car, not looking up more than necessary for fear of seeing Wes again.

Still lacking cable or internet, I tried to pass the time back at my apartment by reading, but couldn't focus. I dug a bottle of whiskey out of a kitchen box and started drinking, not even bothering with a glass. I took another drink each time I started to think about Mark, or work, or Wes, and soon I was buzzed enough to know I would drift to sleep easily. I crawled into bed fully dressed and cried myself to sleep.

The next morning, I again resolved to do better, but I only half-heartedly believed that was even possible. The urge to stay home and wallow in self-pity was much stronger than it had been the day before. But I forced myself to get up and get to work.

My normal classes went well and the students seemed to be at least moderately interested in the assignments. I knew that would only last another week or so, but it felt good at least momentarily to be back in my element in one aspect of my life.

After my final class of the day, I headed to my office and found Lauren waiting outside. I had been relieved to see her in her writing class, and impressed that she'd come having already completed the previous day's assignment that she'd missed.

As I got closer to where she was waiting, however, I realized that something was wrong. Her eyes were red and her face around them slightly swollen. She'd clearly been crying. I didn't want to make her start up again so I decided to try and ignore it.

"Hi. Lauren, right?" I asked.

She nodded and whispered, "Yeah. Do you think I could talk to you about something?"

"Sure, come on in," I said opening my office door and gesturing to a chair. We sat, but she remained looking down, fingers fidgeting with the sleeves of her sweater, leg tapping on the leg of her chair. I tried to break the ice.

"I thought your first two writing assignments were great, Lauren. I think you have a tremendous amount of potential." She didn't respond, she just nodded.

"So did you have a question about the next assignment?" I asked, trying to avoid whatever emotional conflict she was dealing with unless she herself brought it up. "I could maybe find a sample from last semester for you to look at."

She took a deep breath, finally looked up and said, "I'm pregnant."

I set the pen I'd been holding down on my desk and froze. *Why could she possibly be coming to* me *with this?* I thought. *Is this some kind of karmic joke?*

"Oh. Um... How far along are you?" I asked.

"About 11 weeks," she said sheepishly. "I knew I was late, but I was so stressed I just assumed it was that, because that's happened to me before."

I was not in the right headspace or at all qualified to be giving advice to a pregnant student. But what choice did I have with her sitting there across from me?

"I know, we don't really know each other and I've missed half of your class days so far," she continued. "But I don't know anyone here yet, and since I kind of spilled my guts to you in that paper, I figure you know enough about me already that I've got nothing to lose coming to you. I just... I was wondering if you might know where I could go to get some help."

"Well, that really depends on what kind of help you need," I said. "Are you planning to keep the baby?"

"My mother would probably make me tattoo

'whore' on my forehead if I had an abortion and she ever found out," she responded flatly.

"Well, you shouldn't have a child just because it's what someone else wants," I said. "You're an adult. It's your body, and you have the right to choose what happens to it."

"So I've heard," she said with a sly smile on her face. She dug a pack of gum out of her bag, offered me a piece, and took one for herself. "Look, I might be kind of a jerk for this, and even more of one for lying about it upfront, but I overheard some people in class this morning whispering about how you were getting a divorce because of a failed adoption – so... I was hoping you might be able to refer me to an agency?"

I felt like somebody had just punched me square in the chest. I hadn't told anyone about that part of what had happened between Mark and me yet. It had been by far the most painful part of the entire preceding year for me. I had done my best to block it out, desperate not to remember how much it hurt. I scrambled to think who could possibly have found out and spread this information.

Wes. I must have let it slip when I was drunk. Now he's using it to get back at me for rejecting him, I realized. *I could kill him.*

I did my best to not dwell on that in the moment. There was someone there who needed my help. I could at least try to give it.

"Oh," I said, still reeling. "Sure. Just a sec, I'll write down the information for the place we used - well, tried to use."

"Look, I'm really sorry if that's still a sore subject. Like I said, I feel like a real jerk for doing this to you, but I don't know anybody else here. Google was surprisingly not a whole lot of help," she said.

My hands shook as I wrote down the name of the agency that Mark and I had used to try to adopt a child less than a year before. I slid it slowly across the desk, trying to keep my breath even.

"I'm really sorry, but you're saving my ass here," she said. "Thank you."

She picked the slip of paper up off of the desk, and just took off, no regard at all for how what she'd done affected me. *What a fucking nightmare of a week,*

I thought as I staggered out of my office and to my car.

I dropped by Sofia's on the way home. I walked in to find her laughing at the bar with another older woman. She scooted around to the other side of the bar when I approached.

"Don't think I've ever seen you in here twice in one week, blue eyes," she said. "What'll it be?"

"Got a new life back there you can spare?" I joked.

"Well darlin' I'd offer to pour you something stronger'n you are, but by the looks of you I think an empty glass might do that trick," she quipped back. "Rough day?"

"More like year," I said, dropping onto a bar stool.

She rummaged around and pulled a brand new bottle of whiskey from beneath the counter.

"Tell you what *mijo*, take this. Go on home, and get you some rest. This one's on me," she said, sliding the bottle across to me.

"No, Sofia I can't take this," I protested.

"I don't wanna hear it," she said smiling and shaking her head. "Go on."

I didn't have the energy to argue any harder. So I took the bottle and made my way home. When I got there, I collapsed on the sofa and opened the bottle, before realizing I had forgotten to get a glass. I started to get up, thought about the events of the day, and sat back down and took as big a drink as I could handle. I set the bottle down a few times. But then I'd think about the adoption again, and as I'd eventually realize much too late, no amount of alcohol could numb that pain.

Chapter Four | *Mark*

You left the oven on, the house is going to burn down and Adam will die inside, the voice in my head insisted as I reached for the door handle.

No, I told myself. *Adam doesn't live here anymore, and I didn't use the oven today. I'm going out today. I can do this.*

Over the previous month, I'd continued my sessions with Dr. Rodriguez twice a week and started the new medication she'd prescribed. Though I still struggled with my OCD symptoms, I'd been making slow progress. Three weeks into my therapy with her, I'd finally left my house for the first time. I'd only made it a few yards down the block before I'd had to turn around.

I'd convinced myself that people were watching me, judging me, and I wasn't ready to think about that.

Of course, the reality was that the chances that anyone cared what I was doing were very, very slim. But that's just how mental illness goes. It doesn't have to make sense or be anywhere near accurate for your brain to decide that something is true.

When I'd safely made it back inside, I'd reached for my phone to call Adam. I'd been able to force myself to give him space up to that point, but I so badly wanted to share that small victory with him. My heart still ached for him every single day. As much as I needed to heal for myself, I was also doing it because I wanted him back.

Ultimately, I'd decided it wasn't fair to either of us to open that door until I had better progress to report. So, I'd gone out every day since, walking a bit further each time. Even though I was just walking, I was exerting so much mental effort just to quiet the voice in my head telling me to be afraid that I'd feel exhausted as if I'd done an extreme workout by the time I got home each time. It would almost be funny, if it wasn't so devastatingly embarrassing.

Even so, I kept pushing myself. Each day

brought a little more resilience and fewer OCD symptoms. I genuinely felt like I was well on my way to recovery - which brings me to the day in question.

My old law school friend Kate had contacted me to try to schedule lunch together after I'd called her the day Adam left. I had told her that we'd split, but not much else. I was far too embarrassed to admit to my powerful, successful friend that I'd been locked in a battle with my own mind and was losing.

I'd put her off a few times, feeling terrible about lying, but vowing to come clean when I finally saw her in person. I'd finally worked up my radius outside of the house to include a place where we could meet for lunch.

So that's where I was headed on this particular day. To satiate my OCD and stop the images of Adam burning in the house from playing on a loop in my head, I checked the oven knob and opened and closed the door to check for heat seven times before finally leaving the house.

I hadn't yet conquered my mental hang-ups that surrounded driving, so I walked the mile down the road to The Blue Moose Diner. I'd never actually been inside before, but the name was interesting and what I could see through the large display windows seemed cute and cozy. Upon entering, I was greeted by warm colors and soft, peaceful music and lighting, confirming my ideas of the place.

Kate was already waiting at a table when I arrived – punctual as always. She wore the same short haircut she'd had the entire time I'd known her – Kate was the type of person who figured out what she liked and stuck to it – and an expensive looking suit. She stood and greeted me with a firm, but brief hug when I approached. We ordered our drinks and then she looked me dead in the eye and cut right to the chase.

"So, what happened with Adam?"

"Wow, no small talk at all, huh?"

"Time is money, my friend," she said, not a trace of anything but sincerity in her tone.

My mind was filled with images of Adam leaving, getting hurt, and worse. I counted my fingers to compose myself before I took a deep breath and began.

1,2,3,4,5,6,7,8,9,10,1,2,3,4,5,6,7,8,9,10....

"Huh, well, I guess you know my dad died. That was really hard on me. I sort of fell apart." I paused, trying to gauge her reaction. She was listening intently, but seemed to be reserving her reaction for when I finished. So I continued, "But I didn't tell you before that we were also trying to adopt and it didn't work out."

"Oh, my god. I'm so sorry. Sounds like a really rough year. What happened with the adoption?"

"We waited a long time and a woman from L.A. finally picked us. She was due the week after my dad died and we had to fly out to wait for the baby the day after the funeral. But I was just not doing a good job of keeping it together."

"Of course you weren't. You must have been all over the place, emotionally."

"Mostly I was just grieving. Adam was so excited and happy about the baby. I wanted to be too but the mother could see that my heart wasn't in it. It scared her off. Adam didn't speak to me for days after we got home."

"But he knew you'd just lost your father. How

could he blame you?" she whispered, aghast.

"The woman basically did that for him. She made it very clear that were it only Adam, she'd have still gone through with the adoption, but that she was afraid I couldn't be there for the baby," I explained. "And she wasn't wrong. The last year has been really hard. Adam and I fought a lot after that, culminating in me telling him that I didn't even want to adopt anymore. That wasn't true. I was just hurting. I fell into a really deep depression and started having severe OCD symptoms to the point that I stopped working."

"Wait, OCD?" she interjected. "Isn't that just being a neat freak? You should just get a better assistant who will clean for you so you can get back to work. Your career isn't going to wait for you."

"It's a little more complicated than that," I said. "It's, for me at least, been a pretty difficult mental illness to manage."

Good luck trying to explain yourself without sounding like a giant baby, the voice in my head chimed in for the first time since I left the house.

1,2,3,4,5,6,7,8,9,10. I began counting my

fingers

"My doctor told me it varies from person to person," I continued. "For me personally it manifests in violent mental images that I can't get out of my mind no matter how hard I try to distract myself, unless I practice certain behaviors that trick my mind into calming down. And if I don't, I have panic attacks and I feel like I'm going to die. "

"Oh, okay. I get it. So, like there's this beautiful mural across town," she said. "And it's really far out of my way, but sometimes I'll go that far just to see this mural on my way home because it's relaxing. I mean, we all probably have our little things but we can't just drop everything. Maybe you just need to take up yoga or something. Do some meditating between clients – that kind of thing."

Told you you'd sound like a giant baby. She doesn't think it's anything serious at all, the voice mocked.

"Well, I'm not a doctor, but I wouldn't say that driving by a mural is the same thing," I said, the frustration evident in my voice. "I fear for my life if I don't engage in my behaviors and the mental images are disturbing, horrifying things that I wouldn't wish on anyone. But sure, I'll do yoga. That'll solve everything."

I hadn't meant to sound so harsh, but it had just spilled out. Adam had never understood either, and I had accidentally taken that out on Kate. A shocked look flashed across her face, then faded to an angry scowl.

"I'm so sorry. I'm such an ass."

"It's fine," she said curtly. "I know you're going through a hard time." She looked at her phone and feigned interest, but I could see that nothing was on the screen. "Look, I better get going. My assistant says I have a client in my office. But it was good to see you. If you get back to work soon, maybe I'll see you around the courthouse."

"Kate, I'm really sorry," I tried again.

"Don't worry about it. I'll see you." With a quick kiss on the cheek and pat on the back, she was off.

Way to go, dumbass. You really are going to be alone forever now aren't you? It's what you deserve, the voice said.

1,2,3,4,5,6,7,8,9,10.

It's pitiful, really. You couldn't even make it through a simple lunch with an old friend. There's not a chance you'll get Adam back, and God knows no one else could learn to love you at this point.

1,2,3,4,5,6,7,8,9,10,1,2,3,4,5,6,7,8,9,10…

Counting my fingers wasn't working. I was picturing myself rotting away alone in that big house, losing my mind, for the rest of my life. I could feel my chest tightening and knew a full-on panic attack was in the works. I needed to get home. Realizing I didn't have enough time, I decided to head for the restroom and hide to compose myself.

It'll look like you're skipping out on the bill and you'll get arrested and die in jail.

I threw enough cash to cover the bill and a generous tip down on the table and speed-walked to the restroom. I locked myself in a stall, closed the lid to the toilet, and sat on top, pulling my legs up close to my chest.

I tried taking deep breaths and imagining myself

in a peaceful environment - one of Dr. Rodriguez's coping techniques. But no matter what I *tried* to picture, my mind snapped back to me lying dead on the floor of my house, no one ever coming to find me because I scared them all off.

Suddenly, there was a light tapping on the door. I froze and tried to hold my breath, but couldn't stop myself from gasping for air, right on the verge of hyperventilating.

"Hey, buddy, I don't mean to be weird, but do you need some help?" a gentle voice whispered through the crack in the door. "My name is Grayson. This is my diner. I noticed you starting to have a panic attack and wanted to make sure you were okay. But I don't want to intrude, so if you feel like you've got it under control, I'll just go."

He's going to kill you. If you open that door he's going to murder you in cold blood and leave you lying on the floor of this bathroom. I knew that was nonsense, but I still couldn't bring myself to answer him.

"I can hear your breathing and it sounds pretty uneasy, so I'm just gonna stay here for a few minutes, okay?" he said. "I locked the door so no one else can come in, but I don't want to leave in case you get worse and need medical attention. I know you don't know me, but I promise I just want to help. I'm not sure what you need since you can't speak. So for now I'm going to sit right by the door, and I'm going to slide my hand underneath so that you can hold onto it if you need to. Tap the door three times if you want me to call an ambulance. You're not alone, okay?

This is the most embarrassing thing that's ever happened to you. You might as well let yourself hyperventilate and die.

I tried to focus on weighing my options. I had no idea who the person on the other side of that door was, so how could I know he really wanted to help? On the other hand, this was my first time in a public place in over six months and it was not going well at all. If I was ever going to make public outings a regular part of my life again, I needed to get through this panic attack. If someone was really willing to help me do that, what grounds did I have to reject it?

I glanced down at the floor and saw that he'd

indeed slipped his arm underneath the gap in the stall door, but had placed two towels on the ground underneath his hand, almost as if he knew I'd be worried about the germs from the floor.

He knows you're a basket case. He's going to turn you over to a psych hospital.

ENOUGH, I thought to myself. I slowly stepped down, sat on the floor, careful not to touch it with my bare hands, and gingerly took his hand.

"Hi," he whispered gently. Something in his voice was undeniably soothing. I wondered how he knew so much about what I was going through and how to help so effectively. I was shaking slightly, so he tightened his grip, but just barely – just enough to help steady me, but not enough to overwhelm me.

"Can you tell me your name?" he asked.

He wants to know so he can tell the police before they come take you away.

"M-M-Mark," I said between gasps.

"Hi, Mark. My name is Grayson Walker. I'm gonna wait this out with you. I'm right here, okay?"

"O-o-okay," I replied.

"Alright," he said. My breath was starting to level out.

I'm not *alone – at least not right now,* I thought to myself.

We'll see. Your own husband got sick of you. This stranger will too.

"Can I tell you something? I'm really proud of you for accepting help. It takes a lot of courage to be open and vulnerable at a time like this. You're doing great," he said, with another gentle squeeze of my hand.

The kind tone of his voice was calming me down immensely. My breath was almost completely back to normal and my mind was starting to clear up.

"Did you have any pets growing up?" Grayson asked. "I used to have this crazy little pit bull named Oscar. I was a big *Sesame Street* kid, and Oscar the Grouch was always my favorite because he looked so mean but he was always nice to the kids – which is exactly how Oscar the Dog was. He was kind of scary looking, but he was really a big teddy bear. He slept right next to me in my bed every night and greeted me with giant, wet kisses every day when I got home from school."

I smiled at the cute mental image that had now replaced the ones I'd been so afraid of moments before. I was finally able to take a deep, clear breath before I answered him, "That's adorable. I wanted a dog when I was a kid but my dad always said we couldn't afford one. Then I got older and I guess I never felt like I had enough time to be a good owner to one."

"It's sweet that you considered the dog's needs first," he said. "So, Oscar is unfortunately no longer with me after a long, happy life, but I recently rescued a puppy and she's out back. Would you like to meet her? Maybe she can help cheer you up a bit before you head home."

"I don't want to take up any more of your time," I said. "I'm sure you've got better things to do than babysit a grown man hiding in a bathroom stall. I'm so sorry for this, by the way. I'm so embarrassed. But thank you for helping me calm down."

I heard him shift and saw his other hand slip under the door and grasp mine. "Hey, listen. If you take anything away from meeting me today, I want it to be this – don't beat yourself up over things like this. Mental illness is not something to be ashamed of, or to feel guilty for," he said, his voice much more serious, almost stern. "It's not your fault. And you can try to manage it, but that doesn't mean you're always going to be 100 percent in control – and that's okay. The most important thing is that you keep working, and you ask for help when you need it.

"Now, when you're ready to come out, you're more than welcome to come meet Dolly, the cutest golden retriever in the world. But if you'd rather miss out on that, it's totally your call."

I laughed, and finally stood up off of the floor. I took another deep breath, slowly turned the lock, and opened the door to find Grayson still sitting cross-legged on the floor. I offered him my hand and pulled him up.

He looked a lot different than I'd expected based on his gentle voice. I'd later tell him that his appearance was deceiving in the same way Oscar the Dog's must have been. I considered myself pretty tall at six feet, two inches tall, but found myself looking up to meet the piercing gaze of his hazel eyes. He had thick, curly brown hair to match his full, but well-kempt, beard. He appeared to be in his early thirties.

He wore a yellow and blue flannel button-up shirt with the sleeves rolled up, dark blue jeans, and what looked like hiking boots. My first instinct upon taking his full appearance in was to make a joke about him looking like the exact stereotype of a "hipster," but decided I shouldn't risk insulting him after he'd just helped me so much.

"Hi," he said, smiling, large dimples revealing themselves on either side of his mouth along with tiny wrinkles around his eyes.

"Hi," I said back, and before I could say anything more, he pulled me into a hug. He smelled strongly of coffee, but also a light oaky cologne.

"You did great, buddy," he said, then abruptly pulled away. "Oh, sorry, I should have asked before I did that. Are you okay?"

"No, no, it's fine," I said. "Thank you."

He extended a small folded handkerchief to me,

and I just stared at it, puzzled, until I looked up and caught a glimpse of myself in the mirror behind him and saw that tears had started to fall down my face. I was so relieved to be feeling better that I hadn't even realized it. I thanked him and wiped the tears from eyes before trying to offer it back.

"Keep it," he said. "That way, next time this happens you'll have a reminder that somebody cares and wants you to fight through it." He smiled at me again and patted me on the back. "Oh, I should have asked again. Sorry, my instinct to comfort people is to do it with physical reassurance and I totally forget that some people don't care for it."

"No, really, it's okay. I must have serious resting-bitch-face right now," I joked.

"No, you have a great face," he said. We locked eyes awkwardly and he stammered, "No, not a great face - I mean, not that you don't have an attractive face. You do. I just mean – oh boy, I'm gonna shut up now."

He turned bright red until I laughed, and then he relaxed, laughing with me. He led me out of the bathroom, through the diner, out back to a small, quaint cottage set up behind it. I would never have guessed there was an entire residence behind the first building, but there it was, complete with a front yard and a small picket fence. He opened the small door and led me into the yard and then whistled twice. Out of a small pet door near the front door burst a tiny ball of fur. Grayson knelt down and the puppy jumped into his lap and thrashed around in his arms.

"Hi, girl," he laughed. "I missed you too. I brought a new friend for you to meet. Dolly this is Mark. Mark this is Dolly, named of course for the queen of country music." He scooped her up and brought her closer toward me. "You can pet her if you want. She's very friendly."

I carefully reached out and brushed the top of Dolly's head. She squinted one eye and dropped her mouth open into a wide smile as she wiggled in my direction. I opened my arms and he set her gently in them. She wrapped her front paws around my neck and proceeded to smother me in wet dog kisses.

"See? She likes you," Grayson said, beaming.

Dolly began wriggling toward the ground, so I

set her down. She sprinted back inside and quickly returned with something, almost as big as her, between her teeth. She dropped it at my feet and I picked it up to examine it more closely. It was a stuffed moose that showed clear signs of aging. It was a faded blue color, and there were several spots that had been sewn back together. It had two slightly different eyes, as if one had been lost and replaced with the closest available match.

"Oh, no, girl, not this one," Grayson said as I handed him the toy. "Do you want to come in for a cup of coffee or something?" he asked me.

Part of me wanted to just go home and return to the isolation I'd grown accustomed to, but I was in no position to turn down new friends. I nodded and followed him inside. The inside of the cottage was modestly decorated, the furniture mismatched and the walls covered in what appeared to be family portraits.

Grayson offered me a seat and then set the stuffed moose toy on a high shelf, presumably to avoid Dolly reaching it again. He then set about preparing coffee.

"So what do you do?" he asked.

"I'm a lawyer, sort of. I haven't practiced in a little while."

"Oh cool. I wouldn't have guessed. You don't look like the stuffy lawyer type," he replied. "That sounds bad, sorry. I totally meant it as a compliment."

"Thanks, I think. So, do you mind if I ask how you became a pro at coaching strangers through anxiety attacks?" I said.

"That's more of a fourth or fifth date story," he said, setting down a tray with two mugs of coffee and an array of sweeteners and creams. "Um, not that this a date. Sorry, bad joke."

"It's okay," I said, laughing at the sight of his face going bright red again. "In that case, can I ask if the name of the diner has anything to do with that toy? Old childhood favorite?"

His face twisted, almost as if the question pained him. "It's sort of... part of the same story," he said.

"Oh, I'm sorry. I didn't meant to intrude," I said quickly. "Great coffee. Thank you."

"Don't apologize. You know what? You were

really vulnerable with me. Maybe it should be my turn," he said, taking a deep breath. "My little brother, Alex – he had some issues: bipolar disorder, major depression, OCD, general anxiety. After a few years I got pretty good at helping him get through his different mental health crises. That's how I recognized the panic attack, and I wagered on the OCD after I saw you counting your fingers, which is how I landed on distracting you with a happy story. The moose was a gift I picked out for him for one Christmas when we were kids."

"That's really sweet," I said. "He's lucky to have you."

"I guess he was," he said, his voice cracking slightly. "He actually died about ten years ago."

"I'm so sorry," I said. He looked up at me, surprise in his eyes. I looked down to find that without thinking I'd reached out and grabbed his hand. He half smiled at me and squeezed my hand.

"I had been away at school," he said quietly. "My parents let him move out into his own apartment, but he wasn't ready. He ended up living on the street. But he was smart. So smart that he was able to convince my parents everything was fine. But one day he got confused and wandered into a stranger's house. They called the police and a rookie cop got spooked and shot him. I was pretty messed up after that. So, I dropped out of school and came back home. After I had time to recover, I saved up and opened the diner. And I just try to help people as much as I can."

"That must have been awful," I said. "I have to say, I'm impressed at your strength. My father passed recently and, as I'm sure you can tell by what happened back there, I haven't handled it very well."

"Believe me, it wasn't easy," he replied. "I spent a long time on my parent's sofa, even though I blamed them for a while. Alex was my best friend. Without him, I felt like I'd been ripped apart and I was trying to put myself back together but the pieces never quite fit right. It took me a while to adjust. I finally had to realize that he wouldn't have wanted me to let my life pass me by, y'know?"

He carried his empty mug back into the kitchen and returned with a glass of water, Dolly following him back and forth. "It was a couple of years before I finally felt like I could breathe easy again. Even then I felt guilty, like I was leaving him behind. That's why I named the diner after his moose. It's not blatantly morbid, but it honors him."

"I think it's nice," I said. "And the place is great. It's a wonderful tribute to his memory."

"Thank you," he said. "You're very kind."

"So are you," I replied. And I meant it. For the first time since my father died, I was having a real conversation with someone I didn't pay who actually seemed to understand what I was going through and didn't seem to be judging me at all for the way I was dealing with it. And I realized that I hadn't had any problems with troubling mental images or compulsions since we'd left the restroom. Something about him was comforting, peaceful.

"I guess I should get going," I said. "I don't want to take up your whole day."

"Alright, then," he replied, grabbing a business card off of a nearby side table. "Well, listen; if you ever need someone to talk to, or wanna play with the dog, give me a call. If you'll have us, you made two new friends today."

"I'll definitely keep that in mind," I said.

They walked me out and I extended my hand for a shake, but he bypassed it and gave me a quick hug. I knelt down to pet Dolly and then started toward home. I couldn't help feeling proud of myself when I checked the time and realized I'd been out for almost three hours. Even though part of that had been a pretty severe anxiety episode and my lunch with Kate hadn't gone very well, I'd managed to make a new friend and be out twice as long as I'd anticipated.

I took my medication and managed to go the rest of the day without any kind of incident. That night I slept better than I had since Adam left. I so badly wanted to call and tell him how well my day had turned out, but again talked myself out of it.

The next day I had another video appointment with Dr. Rodriguez. I excitedly told her about my outing, and though she was concerned about the panic attack and suggested I try again to patch things up with Kate, she too was proud of the fact that I'd managed to stay away from home for so long and engage with a stranger. She challenged me to speak with Kate and Grayson again when I was comfortable, and to engage with other people as much as possible.

I called Kate a few days later to try to apologize, but she didn't return my call. I couldn't blame her. I had been a jerk. Mental illness or not, she hadn't deserved the way I lashed out. That outburst made me realize that I had been sitting on resentment toward Adam for not being more understanding of what I was going through.

Over the next couple of weeks, I talked through that with Dr. Rodriguez and made a plan to discuss it with Adam when I was finally able to speak with him. Dr. Rodriguez wanted me to meet with her in person in her downtown office a few times, then ask Adam to accompany me. Her timeline put that meeting at two months away, just before Thanksgiving, so I planned to keep working on myself for the next month and reach out to Adam on Halloween if I hadn't heard from him by then.

He'd always loved Halloween, so I knew he'd be in a good mood then. It was the perfect time to give him good news, assuming I still had good news. For the most part, my symptoms had become more manageable. I left the house at least once every day. By the end of September, I'd started doing my own grocery shopping again, but still giving the neighbors' son $20 a week to drive me to the less busy grocery store across town. I hadn't quite worked my way up to driving and couldn't quite handle the large crowd at the store in our neighborhood.

Every once in a while I'd have a rough day that made me question whether I could still win Adam back at all. But I didn't lose hope entirely. I kept the handkerchief Grayson had given me handy as a reminder that I'd made at least one huge stride and had at least one person in my corner. That made it a lot easier to keep working on it.

In the meantime, I began walking to the Blue Moose Diner every Wednesday for lunch and to visit Grayson and Dolly. Grayson and I bonded very quickly over our shared experiences. He'd largely kept to himself after he lost his brother. So, like me, he was happy to have someone who understood him to hang out with. Though part of me worried that he knew too much about me so quickly, I was mostly just grateful to have a friend.

In the first week of October, Grayson called early in the morning. I was afraid to answer, terrified that something had gone wrong. I tried to keep my voice steady as I answered.

"Hey, I'm really sorry to wake you up, but my baker, Chelsea, just quit on me," he whispered. "I remembered you saying you loved to bake and was hoping you might be able to help me out today? I'm gonna try to hire somebody quick, but I can't bake to save my life. I really hate to ask, but you'd be doing me a huge favor. You can eat here free for the next month."

You'll burn the place down. Or you'll just be really terrible at it. Either way, he'll never speak to you again. It's a miracle he's been tolerating you this long.

"I'll be right over," I said, ignoring the voice in my head much more easily than I'd been able to before I restarted therapy.

I spent 10 hours total at the Blue Moose that

day, baking various pastries and even helping to cover tables and the cash register. There were a couple of moments where I thought I might not be able to handle it, but I worked through them. It felt good to actually be doing something productive outside of my own house, and to be helping someone who had helped me. So good in fact, that it gave me an idea.

Grayson had been interviewing candidates to fill the open baker position all day, but didn't seem to be having any luck. When the diner closed for the day, I went back to the cottage and asked him if he'd be willing to let me fill the position, at least temporarily to give him more time to find a better permanent option.

"Are you kidding me?" he responded, cartoonishly grabbing the nearby trashcan and sliding the pile of applications and baked good samples on his table into it. "Buddy, you can work here as long as you want! You really saved my butt today, and not one of these people was anywhere near as talented as you are. I swiped half of the brownies you made for myself before I came home because they were so good."

"Thank you," I said with a huge grin. "I mean, I don't want you to feel obligated or let me do it out of pity. If you really think it's a good idea though, I'd love to do it."

"I don't pity you, Mark. I've actually been really impressed with the progress I've seen you make since we met. Look how long you were here today and you didn't seem to have any major issues. A month ago you were barely getting out of the house. That's amazing. But are you sure? It pays a lot less than a fancy law partnership."

"Oh, good point. I don't know how I'd make it through a work week without access to the golden toilets and unlimited cucumber water from my old office. I guess you should hire whoever made those tragic looking lizard cupcakes," I joked.

"I'm pretty sure it was supposed to be Kermit the Frog," he said, laughing. "But seriously, are we doing this? Is that a yes?"

"That's a hell yes," I said. He raised his hand for a high-five. I slapped my hand against his. Dolly, now twice the size she'd been when I met her, barked excitedly. "I guess I'll see you tomorrow then, boss."

I was so excited that I ran all the way home. When I got there, I immediately dialed Adam's number. Everything was going so well, I couldn't wait to tell him any longer. He didn't answer.

He doesn't want anything to do with you. Why should he? You ruined your marriage. He's probably much better off without you.

"No. He's probably just busy. It's a school night. He probably has papers to grade. He'll call back when he can," I said to myself. And I really believed that. I had every reason to be hopeful. Unfortunately, hope doesn't always mean a happy ending.

A week passed. Then another. I was having a blast working at the Blue Moose. I truly enjoyed the work, and I was getting to know some of the regular customers. I was really starting to feel like myself again, even though I was so far from my old environment. But I couldn't help but feel that something was missing – Adam. The leaves had started to show signs that autumn was setting in, and that time of year was always Adam's favorite. It made me miss him even more.

I tried again, and this time, he answered. At least, I thought he did.

"Hey, stranger," I almost shouted, unable to contain my excitement.

"Hey..." an unfamiliar man's voice said.

"Oh, hello," I said, trying not to let my mind run wild. "Who is this?"

"This is Aaron. On Adam's phone. Who is this?" he asked.

Who the hell is Aaron? He already replaced you? You fucked this up even worse than you thought.

"This is his husband," I said. "Well, ex-husband... Is Adam available?"

"He's in the shower right now. I'll let him know you called," he said. And then the line went dead.

In the shower? Yikes. You might as well crawl back in your hole and die.

"No, don't go there. I'm sure it's nothing. I've made new friends; I'm sure he has too. No big deal," I told myself, unsure.

Keep telling yourself that, and it's just going to

hurt worse when he confirms it's his new boyfriend. And you'll be all alone, forever.

I tried to put it out of my mind. Whoever that was had said he'd tell Adam I called. Surely Adam would want to call and explain. Again, my hope proved unfounded.

The rest of October passed without a peep from Adam. On Halloween night, Grayson asked if I'd planned to hand out candy to trick-or-treaters. He suggested it would be a good exercise in conquering my fears of germs and strangers. After much debate with myself, I agreed on the condition that he helped.

He showed up at my house dressed as Superman and brought Dolly, dressed in a dog's Wonder Woman costume, with him and I had a great time watching the two of them interact with the children. I was struck by how similar their personalities were. Dolly easily matched Grayson's happy-go-lucky demeanor and friendliness. It made it easy for me to overcome the things that were running through my mind regarding strangers coming to my door.

It was getting dark, and the trick-or-treaters

were starting to wind down, but I was thinking that this had been the best night I'd had in a long time when I heard my phone ring from upstairs. I went to retrieve it and was surprised to see that it was Adam.

"Seriously?" I asked myself indignantly. I should have been happy. I'd been waiting almost a month for him to call me back, and it had been just over two months total since the last time I saw him. So why wasn't I over the moon that he was calling? I supposed it was because I expected to have a difficult conversation, and I was having a great night and didn't want to end it with a fight.

I knew I had no right to be upset if Adam was seeing someone. We'd both agreed to the separation, however reluctant it may have been on my part. It didn't matter that all of the progress I'd made was out of the hope that I could win him over again. He was free to do whatever he wanted. But I wasn't ready to hear it yet. I silenced the call, turned off my phone, and went back downstairs.

"Everything okay?" Grayson asked, re-entering the house from having been handing out candy on the porch.

"Nothing that can't wait for another day," I said. If only I'd known then what was waiting for me, I might have changed that answer.

Chapter Five | *Adam*

Despite my best efforts to keep my head down and focus on my work, I remained a topic of discussion in the university's rumor mill for the first several weeks of the semester. Balancing the new classes I'd taken over with my original set proved much more difficult than I'd expected. I went to bed late and woke up early most nights, but I still felt like I was drowning. It didn't help that I felt unbearably lonely.

On top of not being able to turn to Mark like I was used to, being around Amy was awkward because of the situation with Wes. Any time he saw Amy and me together, he'd later find her to complain about me to her. She did her best to stay out of it, but after a while I just felt bad for her and started avoiding them both just to save her the trouble.

By the time summer began to give way to fall, I felt completely and utterly alone. I considered reaching out to my family back home, but I didn't have a great relationship with anyone there. I found myself spending more and more time at Sofia's bar. I'd never been much more than a social drinker before, but I couldn't deny that a few glasses of whiskey or wine made it a lot easier to deal with my new reality.

I'd become such a regular fixture at the bar by the end of September that Sofia was probably my closest friend. I suspected she'd figured out how lonely I was when she asked to have a drink with me on a gray evening in early October.

"Think you might be my new best customer, blue-eyes. Should I be worried or should I call you my new drinking partner and pull up a chair?" Sofia's raspy voice called out as she entered from the kitchen.

I threw back the shot in my hand and pulled out the chair next to me.

"Good answer, darlin'," she said. She pulled a bottle out from underneath the bar and wiped dust off it. "You're better off with me anyhow. Aaron here wouldn't know good liquor if it jumped up and bit 'im in the ass," she said waving her hand dismissively at the bartender who had been serving me as he wandered into the back of the bar. "This here is the good stuff."

"Hold on. If you think he doesn't know liquor, why'd you hire him to tend the bar?" I whispered with a laugh.

"Well, look at him, *mijo*," she said as she sat down and lit up a cigarette. "I was all set to hire somebody else then his fine ass walked in. I may be older'n dirt but my eyesight's 20/20."

"Oh my god, you are not even that old, Sofia," I laughed, making a mental note to look more closely at Aaron and evaluate Sofia's opinion of him when he returned.

"You have a point, blue-eyes. I reckon I could still drink your skinny butt under the table at least," she retorted, pouring two shots for each of us.

"Is that so?" I asked.

"I'll tell you what darlin' - you outlast me and you drink free here for a week. I beat you, you clean out my storage room this weekend," she said.

"You're on," I replied.

There's no way I can lose, I thought.

I was dead wrong. An hour and a half later I was slumped over the bar, watching Sofia drink tequila straight out of the bottle without so much as blinking.

"You win," I said, barely coherent.

"Givin' in so soon, darlin'?" she asked before finishing off the bottle and sucking on a lime wedge.

"I think I'm done drinking for the rest of my life," I said, closing my eyes tightly to avoid watching the room spin around me.

"Good, I won't have to worry about ya stealin' nothin' when you come to work this weekend," she said, patting me on the back. "Sit tight, I'll have Aaron drop you at your place."

I heard her walk off and almost dozed off before Aaron laid his hand on my shoulder.

"Miss Sofia says you need a ride home? I can take you on my way," he said.

I started to decline his offer, but I looked up at him and immediately understood what Sofia was talking about. He had dark red hair and a jaw line that could cut glass, softened only by the light stubble forming on his face. His shirt clung to his body in a way that left little to the imagination. He was smiling at me with a giant, blindingly-white smile that would have made me weak in the knees – if I could feel my knees.

And then I blacked out.

I woke up the next morning face down, head throbbing, stomach in knots, with a terrible taste in my mouth – not-so-subtle reminders from my body that I was no longer the appropriate age to be slamming tequila shots on a weeknight. But those quickly became the least of my worries.

A weeknight. Shit. Work, I thought, assessing just how badly I had screwed myself over. I had a huge stack of midterm papers to start grading. I didn't remember how I had even gotten into bed, much less where I might have left my phone to check the time. I felt blindly around and found something else entirely.

Please don't let that be Wes, I thought, realizing

that my hand was touching someone else's arm.

I slowly opened my eyes and turned to face my latest screw up. I thanked every deity I could think of in my hung-over stupor that instead of Wes, I found Aaron, who was somehow even more attractive through sober eyes. That brief second of relief gave way to panic over what he was doing there. Despite being afraid to know, I carefully lifted the blankets, trying not to wake him.

Surprisingly, I found us both to be fully clothed. I hoped we had stayed that way all night. Even more surprising was that in place of immediate guilt over possibly having slept with Aaron, I had instead found myself feeling a bit disappointed to have been blackout drunk when it happened.

I guess I'm just leaning into this single thing then, I thought. *Amy would be proud... I think... maybe not.* I remembered somewhat hazily how good the shirt he was wearing had looked on him the night before. *Yeah, she'd definitely be proud.* I should have felt guiltier. I knew that. But it had been almost two months since I'd moved out, and I'd be lying if I said it wasn't nice to not wake up alone for a change, regardless of what had actually happened the night before.

I finally found my phone –no, his phone - under my pillow and checked the time. 6:08 a.m. – I had a solid two hours before I needed to head out for my first class. I slowly slid out of bed, trying my best not to disturb the unreasonably attractive sleeping man in my bed.

I regretted standing up pretty much instantly. *You're too old for this shit,* I reminded myself. I stumbled to the kitchen and started a pot of coffee to brew while I drank as much water as I could handle. I pulled the first paper off of the top of my stack to start grading. Three attempts at reading the opening paragraph yielded no discernible thesis statement, so I knew the rest of it would be a waste.

Just pass them, I told myself. I marked a big red "C" on the paper and set it aside. The next paper started off stronger, and in fact was so well researched that my hung-over brain was having a hard time. I should have been able to at least minimally comprehend what I was looking at, but with my head throbbing and my eyes burning, it was hard to even get through one line of the text.

I decided to try to wake myself up a bit first. So, I drank a cup of coffee as quickly as I could without burning myself, and ran a shower. I closed my eyes and let the hot water run down my body, breathing in slowly. I almost started to think about Mark, but I heard movement in the bedroom and snapped out of it. I quickly finished up my shower, dressed, and went into the kitchen to find Aaron rummaging around in a cabinet.

"Morning," he said. "Thought I'd make some breakfast."

"I don't mean to be rude, but I've gotta get going," I said.

"Aw, already?" he asked, playfully pouting. "I'm never up this early since I work so late. I was hoping you could show me what exactly it is that mornings have to offer." I laughed and he smiled that overwhelming smile again. "I'm serious, bro. The term 'morning person' has always seemed like a fucking oxymoron to me."

"Look I'm sorry, I feel like I need to address the big drunk elephant in the room," I said, bracing myself for the answer. "Did we, um, you, know..."

"Fuck?" he asked nonchalantly. "Nah, dude. I helped you get settled and then realized the game was in overtime and you offered to let me watch it. I guess I passed out after it was over. That's a great mattress."

"Oh, thank god," I said, relived of the guilt I had just barely even been feeling.

"Damn," he said, freezing with a frying pan in his hand. "Am I that ugly?"

"No," I practically shouted. "I didn't mean it like that. It's just-"

"Dude, I'm just fucking with you. You told me a little about your situation last night. Sounds pretty fucked," he said.

"Yeah... Something like that," I admitted.

"Well, then you need a day off. Come on, what would normal people do with an entire day where they woke up this early and didn't have any responsibilities?" he asked, coming around the bar to stand right in front of me.

"Well, if we were a straight couple in a romantic comedy, we probably would have actually slept together. So now we'd lie in bed with the sheets strategically covering our more intimate body parts and I'd be drawing circles in your chest hair like a lovesick teenager; and we'd both be thinking about how perfect the other one is even though we've literally known each other for five minutes and you were trying to close down my cute independent book shop, or writing an article about me without asking, or whatever the convoluted set up was," I said, trying to be funny.

"Dude, I can't honestly say I understand all of that, but parts of it sound kind of nice," he said, moving in close. "Come on, man. When's the last time you just took a day – the whole day – and had some fun?"

I considered his question and legitimately couldn't answer. For at least the last year all of my free time had been spent on trying to care for Mark, until I left him. Then it had been spent trying to clean up my messes. I hadn't missed a single day of work in my entire career. What harm could it do?

"I make really good bacon," he said in a singsong voice, taking my hands and swaying them back and forth slightly.

"Isn't all bacon good bacon? Also how would you know if you're never up early?" I asked, laughing, trying my hardest not to give in to his charm.

"Dude, bacon is an all-day food. But your first point can only really be tested by you sticking around and letting me try to prove that I do in fact make better than average bacon," he retorted, loosening his grip just enough to make me want it back.

I thought about the giant piles of class materials sitting on my table, then about all of the things I would much rather be doing than trying to make sense of the nonsense that I knew most of the students had thrown down on paper without a second thought. I looked back at Aaron and saw him grinning excitedly, as if he already knew what I was about to say.

"I mean, as an academic, what choice do I have but to test your theory?" I said, surprised by how excited he seemed to be to have won me over.

"You're on," he said, scurrying back into the

kitchen.

As I watched him start cooking and drafted an email to my classes to give them the day off, it hit me that this was the first time in ages that I'd felt like someone was truly interested in me and enjoyed being in my company. That made me feel sad for how far my marriage had fallen, but it mostly made me feel hopeful for the future.

Everything's gonna be okay, I thought. And finally, after months of feeling lost, I was starting to believe that. As I watched Aaron move around the kitchen, I was reminded of Mark. He'd always loved being in the kitchen. It was his favorite room in the house.

I'd heard from one of my old neighbors that he had been going for walks in the area over the last month. I was so proud of him that I'd nearly cried. I wanted to call, or go to him and tell him how proud I was. But Amy had pointed out that giving him any kind of hope that we could get back together before I was absolutely sure could set him back.

And I was nowhere near sure. My pregnant

student, Lauren, had indeed gone to the adoption agency that Mark and I had tried to use, and because she was in two of my classes, I had to see her every single day. And each time, I remembered the particularly nasty fight I'd had with Mark in which he'd shouted at me that he didn't want to adopt anymore – that he had only even agreed to it in the first place because he knew had badly I'd wanted it, but he didn't want to be a father, especially now that he'd lost his.

That had been the point of no return for me. I'd tried to continue being supportive of him, but my heart was broken. I felt more like a caregiver than a partner in a marriage. I'd become so lost in those memories that I didn't immediately notice when Aaron set down a plate of food at the table and sat next to me.

"If you let it get cold, you're going to fuck up the results of the experiment," he said with a chuckle.

"Sorry, my head was somewhere else."

"No way, dude. None of that today," he chided "Today is about having some goddamn fun and cancelling the pity party you've been throwing yourself. Today we party for real. Deal?"

"Deal," I said, taking a drink of what I thought was just orange juice from a glass he'd set in front of me. It had a strong shot of vodka mixed in. "Whoa, little early isn't it? What was wrong with plain orange juice?"

"It is orange juice. It's just grown-up orange juice," he said. "Think of today as a vacation. This is part of the experience."

"I guess you're the boss."

"Damn straight," he said, laughing. "So, the bacon. Was I right, or was I right?"

"I've had better," I said with a smirk after taking a bite.

"Shut up," he said, laughing as he threw a dish towel at me. "You're full of it."

We finished breakfast and he helped me clean up. When we were done, he suggested heading down to the pier for a walk and then to the beach for a swim. When I reminded him the water had probably turned cold as summer faded, he reminded me that I'd said he was the boss. I couldn't argue with that.

We stopped by the bar on the way to check for

my phone. But it hadn't been turned in. I almost asked him if he minded if we stopped to pick up a replacement from the carrier's store, but remembered the day was supposed to be about fun and decided it could wait. After all, it hadn't exactly been ringing much.

We drove down to the pier and walked down the row of booths run by local farmers and merchants. Aaron bought a giant touristy hat and when I started to walk ahead, put it on my head and laughed.

"I think you're forgetting how much older than you I am," I said, adjusting the hat. "I'm at peak dad age right now. I can absolutely get away with wearing this."

"True enough," he said, a sly smile creeping across his face. "With a face like that you can get away with a lot."

My cheeks flushed and I turned away to hide it, but I knew he saw. "So, are we swimming, or what? We need to get swim trunks."

"No, we don't," he said, walking ahead. "Trust me."

He led me much further down the beach than I had ever been, over a large rock formation to a deserted cove.

"I had no idea this was here," I said.

"I know. Most people don't. Beautiful isn't it?"

"It's breathtaking," I said, noticing that the water was much cleaner here than the rest of the beach, the sand unmarried by unsightly beach chairs or trash.

"Reminded me of you," he said.

I turned my attention from the water to look at him and realized he had completely stripped down. I fought to keep my eyes locked on his face as I asked, "What the hell are you doing?"

"Going for a swim. You coming?"

"No, no, no, no," I said. "Nuh-uh, not happening."

"Suit yourself," he said, running toward the water. It was hard not to watch him. His body was well toned, a thin layer of light red hair covering most of it. He waded in until the water was at his knees, then dove forward. I was dumbfounded by how free spirited he was.

And then I realized I wanted to be that way too. I hesitated for a brief moment, then saw him emerge from the water, pure joy on his face. I quickly took off my clothes and ran toward the water. He stood up and smiled at me, until I stopped dead in my tracks at the edge of the water.

This is nuts. What are you doing? I thought to myself. Then I looked up and saw Aaron splashing around, free and wild as if the rest of the world didn't matter. *Screw it.* I ran forward and dove in near where he was. I laid my head back and let myself float on the water.

As small waves crashed over me, I closed my eyes and finally let myself relax. I felt completely weightless, as if the waves were washing away all of my stress, heartache, guilt, and regret. My ears were submerged and all I could hear was the magnificent crashing of the ocean. It made all of my problems seem small, which was a blessing of the highest order. I had never before been so grateful to feel insignificant.

I felt a smile spread across my face, and not the cursory smile I'd grown so accustomed to wearing to avoid people knowing anything was wrong. This was a genuine, happy, smile like I hadn't felt in ages. I didn't know whether to laugh or cry, but before I could even try to decide I was doing both.

I stood up and pulled Aaron into a tight embrace. "Thank you," I said through tearful laughs. "You have no idea how badly I needed this."

"See?" he said, grinning from ear to ear. "I'm full of good ideas. Stick with me, Humpty Dumpty. We'll get you back together in no time."

His face turned mischievous and he splashed water all over my face. I splashed him back, and he lunged forward and tackled me into the water, initiating a playful wrestling match. There was a small concern in the back of my mind that this was inappropriate, but I was really having fun. It had been way too long since I could honestly say that. So I quieted that concern, and we spent the rest of the morning frolicking in the ocean like children without a care in the world.

As noon approached, dark gray clouds began forming in the area, so we got dressed and headed back to my apartment, picking up lunch on the way. Over giant, greasy burgers from what Aaron called, "the best place in the Americas," we talked more and I learned a lot about him.

He was 28 and an aspiring theater actor, bartending now to save up money to move to New York. Like me, he came from a large family and was the oldest of four siblings. He was Aaron the third, but didn't use the suffix because, also like me, he wasn't close to his father. I probably wouldn't have remembered all of the little details of what he was telling me, if it hadn't been for the charming way he spoke. His smile was contagious, and he spoke with such animation and gusto that it was hard not to hang on his every word.

After lunch, he took me bowling at a tiny bowling alley in a part of town I didn't even know existed. I played so badly the first game that he had the attendant put up bumpers as a joke. But I used them anyway and still lost the second game.

When we left the bowling alley, the rain we'd been worried about earlier in the afternoon had arrived. It was raining so hard that we decided it was best to retire back to my apartment for the day, where we watched bad reality TV for several hours. After a while, I caught him staring at me.

"Do I have something on my face?" I said, wiping at my cheek.

"No, dude," he said laughing. "I was just thinking that I've seen you at Sofia's every night since I started working there. But today is the first time I've seen you smile. Not bad for a first date, right?"

I felt my cheeks flush bright red. *Oh shit,* I thought. I hadn't meant for this to be a date, and I hadn't until that moment considered the implication of having embraced him when we were both fully nude. I hadn't meant it as anything other than appreciation for what he'd done for me.

But he was also so damned handsome. His hair was still wet from the beach and the rain; and he'd changed into one of my t-shirts, which fit pretty loosely on him, while we washed the beach water and sand off of his clothes. It all played into the relaxed vibe that made him so appealing. It was getting harder to deny that I was attracted to him.

"Is that – um, is that what this was?" I asked, trying not to let on how nervous I suddenly was.

"Depends," he said, scooting just slightly closer, that smile flashing at me again.

"On what?" I asked, my entire body tensing up.

"You a kiss on the first date kinda guy?" he asked, a distinct glint in his eye that spelled trouble.

"No, not usually," I said, sweating bullets.

"Then, let's not consider this a date," he said, leaning in further. I felt like I was frozen in time as I watched his face approach mine. My body was screaming at me to let it happen, but my mind delivered a resounding no. I stood up off the couch before his lips could reach mine.

"I'm sorry," I said. "I can't do this. I'm married."

"Bro, aren't you getting a divorce?" he asked.

"Well, yes," I conceded. "But I haven't even filed the paperwork yet, and I've heard my husband has been getting better. So-"

"So, why do you still live here alone and get drunk every single night?"

"I do not get drunk every night,"

"Yeah you do, man. I've seen you come in to the bar every night for the last two weeks, and every night you take an Uber home because you're too shitfaced to drive yourself. So either you're an alcoholic, or you don't want to go back to your husband."

"Hey, you don't know me just because we spent one day together," I said, almost shouting.

"Whoa, bro, calm down. It's not that serious," he insisted. "I misread the vibe. No big deal. I'll leave." He started cleaning up the various snacks he'd gathered while we were watching TV.

"Wait, you don't have to go," I said. I'd realized that I'd only gotten angry because there was truth to his words, as much as it pained me to admit. "You're right, okay? There is a part of me that doesn't think I should go back to Mark now, if ever. But there is still an equal part of me that loves him, and hopes that he gets better so we can be together again. And I already fucked up once, and the guilt eats at me every day. I just don't want to make the same mistake twice."

"Understood," he said plainly, setting down what he had gathered. "How about we forget the last five minutes happened, have a drink, and try to relax?"

Five beers later I was enthralled in another of his stories. Before I knew it, midnight was approaching. I was amazed by how easy it was to spend an entire day with Aaron, but even more by how easy *everything* about him was. We could have had a huge fight and gone our separate ways. But he conceded so easily and just let it roll off his back. He did whatever he wanted without any concern. He just dealt with any consequences that arose, no hand-wringing whatsoever.

He spent the night again that night, on the couch this time. That weekend, after I fulfilled my lost bet duty to clean out Sofia's storage room at the bar, he went home with me again. One night turned into two, turned into three, and he was still there two weeks later. He left every day for work at the bar and to get fresh clothes from the apartment he shared with three other people, but every night ended with us drinking together and him passing out on the couch. He didn't try to make a move again, and I wasn't so lonely anymore. So, I didn't mind him crashing.

Unfortunately, that saying about hindsight being 20/20 is 100 percent correct. If I could go back and undo every bit of October of that year, I would. As it stands, my new friendship with Aaron was a catalyst for chaos in both my personal life and my professional life.

It started innocently enough. In those first two weeks he stayed at my apartment, I missed three more days of work. After the third, Dr. Lewis informed me that while she understood that I was going through a tough time, any further days missed in that term would result in my pay being docked. But by that point I had begun to adopt Aaron's laissez-faire attitude, and I missed work again the very next day.

Until that day, I'd been so immersed in my new carefree lifestyle that I hadn't even replaced my missing cell phone. I finally got a replacement that day, only because I realized my next bill was coming due and I figured I should have a phone if I was paying for it. That was the only logical thing I did that day.

When I returned from buying the phone, Aaron was waiting at my apartment with several bottles of liquor and a large pack of beer. He'd gotten the lead role in a local production of *Hamlet* and wanted to celebrate. It was only 2 in the afternoon, but it wasn't like I had anywhere to be.

We spent the afternoon drinking much more than normal. At some point, once I was well past the legal blood alcohol limit, I became preoccupied with thoughts of that first day when he'd tried to kiss me. I was kicking myself for not letting him.

He was talking about how excited he was about the play, and I was watching his mouth move, wanting to kiss him more and more with each time he licked his lips or bit the corner of his bottom lip as he thought of what to say next.

Maybe it was the six shots of whisky. Maybe it was the four beers I'd chased them with. Maybe it was just that he was sexy and I was an idiot. Whatever the case, I found myself inching closer. He smelled incredible, notwithstanding the liquor on his breath. If I'm honest, that might have actually helped. He was still wearing the clothes he'd warn to his audition – a blue dress shirt that nicely accentuated his arms and contrasted his golden hair, and a tight pair of black slacks. I didn't stand a chance. I poured two shots of whiskey and drank them both.

"Dude, are you okay?" he asked.

"Let's not consider this a date," I said, recalling the line he'd tried on me that first night as I poured each of us another shot.

He looked confused for a split second, then a sly grin spread across face and he took the shot. He handed me mine and I drank it quickly as he leaned across the table and my heart began to pound. He placed one hand on the back of my head and pressed his lips against mine. I briefly hesitated, but kissed him back. He moved closer and straddled my lap as he kissed me again and again.

I ran my fingers through his long hair as the kissing grew more intense and passionate. He began kissing my neck and every nerve ending in my body was ignited. I wrapped my arms around his thighs and stood, lifting him with me. He grabbed a bottle of tequila as I carried him to the bedroom and collapsed back on to the bed with him on top of me.

He took a drink straight from the bottle and then passed it to me. I took a large swig and dove right back in to kissing him. This devolved into perhaps the clumsiest sex of my life. We were much too drunk for it to be considered "good" but it was fun nonetheless.

Afterward, I lay with my head on his chest, exhausted, his arms wrapped around me. "Is this the romantic comedy bullshit you always dreamed of?" he said, playfully tickling me.

"Fuck you," I said, attempting to return the tickling, but giving up quickly.

"Didn't get enough the first time?" he asked with a laugh. "I think you're gonna have to buy me dinner if you wanna go again, dude."

"Shut up," I said, laughing and slapping his chest. "You know where the fridge is. Eat up while I take a shower."

"Yes sir," he said, mischievously. "Be bossy like that next time, Dr. King."

I rolled my eyes and got up to take a shower, thinking I should at least consider getting some work done. I was still *very* drunk, so I hoped a hot shower would wake me up a bit. I let the hot water run over me. I started to wonder if I'd make a mistake – if I'd wake up feeling guilty in the morning.

Who cares, I decided. I heard my phone ring from the bedroom and I was instantly sure that it was Mark. I had briefly wondered if he'd called while I was without a phone earlier in the day, but decided he probably hadn't. But karma would serve me right for him to call now. I hurriedly exited the shower and toweled off, but the ringing had stopped. I could hear muffled talking as I made my way to the kitchen where Aaron was.

"I'll let him know you called," he said as he hung up the phone.

"Who was that?" I asked. "Also, you answered my phone?"

"Sorry, reflex," he said with a shrug. "It was a wrong number anyway."

"Wrong number? But you told them- oh, oh, hello," he'd cut me off my kneeling in front of me and kissing my stomach, slowly moving lower.

"Bro, I can either keep talking or I can put my

mouth to better use," he said. His warm breath blowing over my stomach felt like electricity. He was making it hard to think about anything else. "Your call."

I closed my eyes and gave in. I wouldn't think about the call again until it was too late.

Over the next couple of weeks, Aaron migrated from sleeping on the couch to sleeping in my bed. I made it to work every day, but I was simply going through the motions, recycling old assignments, arbitrarily assigning grades. I stopped attending my scheduled office hours. Lauren tried to schedule an appointment with me several times but I knew she probably had more questions about the adoption agency rather than actual class, so I cancelled each time.

On Halloween night, the university's English department held a small get together for the faculty and graduate students. Amy had organized it, but I didn't want to go because I knew Wes would be there. But I wanted to support Amy, and I knew Dr. Lewis would be on my case even more if I didn't show up. But there was no rule that said I had to go alone.

Aaron and I arrived a half hour late. We'd

agreed to arrive late after "pre-game" drinks, then leave as early as possible. Maybe I was imagining it, but I could swear every eye was on the two of us as we entered hand-in-hand. Out of the corner of my eye I saw Wes make a beeline for Amy, who was trying to help Jason wrangle their kids into a table in the corner of the room.

"Is that the guy that's pissed because you wouldn't fuck him again?" Aaron asked.

"Is it that obvious?" I asked.

"Let's have some fun," he said, winking.

He grabbed two cups of punch from the nearby table and then angled himself away from the crowd as he produced a flask from the inner pocket of his jacket and poured tequila into each cup. I should have stopped him. But I drank the punch, grabbed the flask and refilled my empty cup with straight tequila, then drank that.

Aaron smiled and shook his head, as if to say he was impressed. He led me nearer to where Wes was angrily gesticulating at a very bored looking Amy. Without saying a word, Aaron grabbed me and dipped me backward as he planted a huge kiss on me. Wes stormed off, even more angry than he'd been before. Amy awkwardly shuffled back to where Jason was sitting with their son and daughter. Aaron thought it was hilarious. I almost agreed with him, until I saw Dr. Lewis heading my way.

"Dr. King," she said sternly. "I need to speak with you, please. In my office- *now*." I followed her to her office, frantically cramming a piece of gum in my mouth to try to mask the tequila on my breath.

"Sit," she said. The lack of pleasantries told me I was screwed. Ana was not one to skip pleases and thank yous. "We need to discuss the way that you have behaved over the last two months, Dr. King – your display in there being merely the latest in a string of actions that display seriously poor judgment."

"It was just a kiss," I said, shifting awkwardly in my seat. "I'm a grown man. He's a grown man. Is that the real problem here?" Big mistake. I knew that was a huge reach.

"You know very well that it isn't," she said. Her voice had raised sharply. "The problem is that you were very clearly trying to get a rise out of Mr. Harris, which you successfully did. Have you forgotten that Mr. Harris is still a student of this university? A student you have had a sexual relationship with that was broadcast all over campus-"

"Yeah, by *him,*" I interjected. "Among other very private details of my personal life."

"That only further proves my point, Dr. King," she said, her face twisting in frustration. "You had the poor judgment to share intimate details of your life with a student who is known for his lack of discretion. Now you miss entire days of work with no valid excuse. You haven't held office hours in almost a month, and several students have complained that your grading system seems entirely arbitrary. After investigating I'm inclined to agree.

"And I hope you don't think one stick of wintermint is covering the overwhelming smell of alcohol on your breath. When was the last time you came to this campus entirely sober, without a hangover? I suspect the answer is over a month ago and I cannot allow you to continue on my staff this way."

"Wait, am I being fired?" I asked, my breath suddenly shallow and uneven.

"No, Dr. King," she said, sighing heavily. "I understand that you have had a very difficult year. And until this semester you have been a very reliable and valuable member of my staff. I will not terminate your employment for coping poorly when life dealt you an undesirable hand. I am, however, going to put you on suspension – effective immediately."

I opened my mouth to protest, but she put up a single finger, signaling for me to remain silent. "You may return at the beginning of the spring semester, provided that you can prove to me that you are sober, and prepared to work with a renewed focus."

I sat in stunned silence. I knew I hadn't been giving 100 percent of my capability to work, but had it really gotten that bad?

"That will be all, Dr. King. Please, I implore you to seek out assistance for your alcoholism," she said.

"I'm not an alcoholic," I insisted, realizing that was the second time in one month I'd uttered those words.

"Oftentimes, Dr. King, it is difficult for us to see ourselves not as we wish to be, or as we remember ourselves, but as we have become," she said solemnly. "I believe if you engage in true introspection, you'll come to a different conclusion. I truly hope to see you in January. Please get home safely."

She gestured to the door and I was too dumbfounded to say anything else. I stumbled down the hallway and stood in the doorway to the room where the party was being held. Amy spotted me first. She gave me an apologetic look that told me she knew and worse, she pitied me. I met Aaron's gaze and gestured for him to follow me out.

He made a big show of being angry and indignant on my behalf when I told him what had happened, but everything around me was like white noise. I fished the flask out of his jacket pocket and we split what was left. As if everything else I'd done in the month prior hadn't been stupid enough, I got into the passenger seat of his car and we set off toward my apartment.

The next thing I remember is a dull aching in my ears as I awoke to an unbearable noise. An ambulance, sirens blaring in the distance. No, I was in the ambulance. A bright light in my eyes, back and forth. Searing pain in my left arm. Throat burning. Something on my face – an oxygen mask. *Oxygen. I'm alive,* I thought. *Oh god, where is Aaron?*

I frantically tried to sit up, but the paramedics pinned me down. I could hear them speaking to me, but couldn't make out what they were saying. Someone grabbed my left arm and pain exploded throughout it so fiercely that I blacked out.

I awoke in a hospital bed some time later. My head was throbbing. I tried to assess my injuries. My left arm was broken, and there was what felt like a nasty gash on my forehead, but everything else seemed fine, aside from minor cuts and bruises. I was relieved for a split second, then realized I didn't know where Aaron was.

I pressed the nurses' call button repeatedly out of desperation. The nurse who responded explained to me that Aaron was fine. He had no major injuries, but had been arrested for driving under the influence. He had driven right into a traffic light pole, and the light fixture itself had fallen through the windshield, crushing my left arm. Luckily, we were the only car involved and no one else was injured.

I was overcome with guilt. Aaron wouldn't have been in jail if I had just skipped the stupid party, or if he just hadn't gotten involved with me in the first place. I was starting to face the fact that I might in fact be an alcoholic when the nurse asked if there was someone else they could call for me.

"What do you mean, 'someone else'?" I asked.

"Well, sir, the paramedics found your cell phone on the scene and we tried to contact the emergency contact you'd programmed. But the first call wasn't answered and there were a few attempts after that went straight to voicemail," he explained.

I declined and thanked the nurse and he left me alone. I had programmed Mark as the emergency contact when I'd gotten the new phone without thinking. *Why wouldn't he answer?* I thought to myself. *Multiple calls and he wasn't concerned?*

I knew Mark had been working toward getting better in the hopes of us getting back together. So I couldn't come up with a reasonable explanation for why he would suddenly not care if I called, but I intended to find out. The next morning, after I'd been questioned by the police and discharged from the hospital, I took a taxi to my old house.

There was a car that I didn't recognize in the driveway. *Early for visitors,* I noted to myself. I rang the doorbell and waited. No one answered. I rang it again and waited a few more minutes. Still nothing. I walked over to one of the large windows that looked in on the living room and peaked in through a gap in the curtains.

Mark was there, asleep on the couch. *He was always a heavy sleeper,* I recalled. *Maybe he's just been asleep this whole time. No, doesn't explain the calls going straight to voicemail after the first.* And then I noticed something strange – what looked like a dog resting with its head in Mark's lap. I craned my neck to try to get a better view, and realized that lying down next to Mark and what was indeed a dog, was another man.

He couldn't answer the phone because he was with this guy? I thought, unreasonably offended. In hindsight, I know I had no right to be angry. After all, I was just in a car accident with a man who had practically become my live-in boyfriend, or at the very least, live-in friend with benefits.

But when you love someone as much and as long as I loved Mark, and when you're as big an alcoholic as I had unwittingly become, logic goes out the window. Unlike the large rock I found in the front yard, which went right *through* the window.

Shit's about to hit the fan, I thought as I came to my senses. And boy, was that the understatement of the century.

Chapter Six | *Mark*

There was a brief moment when I awoke on the first morning of November where I thought I surely must still be dreaming. I heard a large crash, then an even larger thud. I snapped awake along with Grayson and Dolly both of whom, like me, must have fallen asleep on the sofa during the movie we were watching the night before.

Someone's here to murder you, and your new friends. They're dead because of you. Way to go.

I quickly counted my fingers to try to quiet my mind.

1,2,3,4,5,6,7,8,9,10

Then I looked over to the bay window across the room and saw him through a large hole in one of the panes. *Adam*, wearing a cast on his left arm, visibly angry. Dolly began barking loudly near the window and

Grayson jumped off of the sofa and stood in front of me, as if he were trying to protect me.

"Are you okay?" he asked. I nodded. "Do you have any idea who this guy is?"

I stood and tried to get a closer look at Adam, unsure if I was even seeing him correctly. He looked very different from the last time I'd seen him. His normally clean-shaven face had an uneven smattering of stubble. His hair had grown quite a bit and was wholly unkempt, a jarring contrast from his usual neat style. His eyes looked bloodshot and there were large bags underneath them. I wasn't honestly sure I *did* have any idea who he was.

He came to kill you. He left you and he found someone better. Now he's going to kill you because he hates you. My chest tightened and I couldn't fight the mental images working their way in – Adam standing angrily over my limp body, me bleeding out on the floor.

"Mark? Mark, I'm here," Grayson said. I felt his hand gently grip my arm and snapped back to reality.

"I'm sorry," I said through tense breaths. He

nodded at me reassuringly. "It's – it's my husband. It's Adam."

"What? Are you serious? You haven't heard from him since he left. Why is he throwing rocks through your window?"

"I don't know," I admitted. "But I'm going to find out. You can go if you want. I'll do my best to be at work at the diner on time."

"I'm not leaving you," he said firmly. "He doesn't seem like he's in a good head space right now. I don't feel comfortable leaving you here alone with him. I'll take Dolly and go upstairs, but I'll be right up there if you need me."

"Grayson," I started, but his face was the most serious I'd ever seen it. He squeezed my arm gently, scooped Dolly up into his arms and went upstairs.

Should have asked him to stay. You're as good as dead now.

1,2,3,4,5,6,7,8,9,10… "No, this is fine. Adam would never hurt me. We're just going to talk," I told myself. I carefully walked around the broken glass and opened the front door.

"Adam," I said breathlessly. "What, um… what's going on?"

"That's a great question, Mark," Adam said aggressively, storming up the steps to meet me face to face. "Here's one for you: why the fuck didn't you answer your phone last night? Too busy playing house with whoever the hell that is?"

I'd planned to try to calmly talk and figure out what was going on, but he was clearly not interested in that approach. His breath reeked of alcohol, and I couldn't help but wonder if that had anything to do with his behavior and appearance. Neither of us had ever been big drinkers, but his father had a serious drinking problem before finally dying from liver failure a few years before. Regardless, I wasn't going to just sit back and not defend myself after all this time.

"Wait, are you really mad that I didn't answer the phone? I've called you twice this month. You didn't answer the first time, and another man answered the second. You didn't call me back either time. Why should I have to answer your calls? And *that,*" I said, pointing upstairs toward where Grayson had gone, "is my boss. I got a job, which you'd know if you'd returned either of my calls. But I guess you were too busy with Aaron, or whatever his name is."

"I didn't get either of those calls Mark. I lost my phone and didn't have one for a while, and Aaron never told me you called. And he's just a friend," he said, rubbing his neck with his good hand on the last bit.

"Just because we've been separated for a couple of months doesn't mean I've forgotten everything I know about you. You always rub your neck when you lie, Adam," I said.

The situation was getting out of control, not that it hadn't started that way, what with the broken window and all. I took a deep breath, rubbed my temples, and tried to continue in a calmer manner. "Look, I don't even care. You left me, right? I shouldn't have expected you not to see other people. I do, however, feel like I should have been able to expect you not to throw a rock through my window bright and early in the morning. What is the matter with you? And what happened to your arm?"

"I was in a fucking car accident, Mark," he said.

"It wasn't me calling last night. It was the hospital."

Way to go jerk. You threw away any chance you ever had of not dying alone because he didn't return your calls. He's never going to take you back now and you're going to be lonely and miserable for the rest of your life.

"Oh god, Adam I'm so sorry. I had no idea. Are you… okay?"

"No, I'm not fucking okay, Mark.

"Sorry. Do you want to come in?" I asked.

He rolled his eyes and strolled past me with his arms crossed. He looked around the foyer and living room suspiciously, as if he expected to find some evidence of impropriety on mine and Grayson's part.

"So, your *boss* sleep here often?" he asked haughtily, making air quotes as he said the word "boss".

"He *is* my boss, Adam, just a friend. And no, he doesn't. He came over to help me hand out candy to trick-or-treaters so that I wouldn't be so afraid to do it. We were watching a movie afterward. It got late and we must have fallen asleep. That's it, I swear."

"So that's it? You were watching a movie, so you couldn't be bothered to answer the phone? Fucking the guy would have been a better excuse."

"No. I didn't answer the phone because I was hurt. You hurt me Adam," I said. He scoffed and rolled his eyes, still scanning he room diligently. "Have you already forgotten that *you* walked out on *me?*"

"You know it wasn't that simple, Mark," he said, whirling around. "I tried so hard to stay, to make this work; but you, you just…"

"I what, Adam? I didn't recover from my grief on your timetable? I didn't lose my father and bounce right back? What Adam? I what?" I demanded.

"You quit trying," he shouted. "You stopped going to therapy. You stopped seeing me. I was just your babysitter by the end."

He's right. You're a huge loser.

"No, that's not fair, Adam," I responded, as much to myself as to him. "I kept taking my medication. I kept trying. You know damned well that I didn't just stop going to therapy. I stopped going *anywhere*. I couldn't leave the house. It wasn't my choice, Adam. I was sick. I still am."

"You look fine to me, Mark," he said, his voice growing louder still. "I move out and suddenly you're leaving the house and working? Why the fuck couldn't you do that when I was here?"

"I *tried,* Adam," I yelled back. "And you're acting like I just decided to be better one day. I didn't. It took me a lot to work up to even going outside, much less walking down the street far enough to get a job. And the only reason I can even have this job is because I managed to stumble into the one place that has an owner who actually understands what I've been through and why there are days when I just can't make it to work, or days when I can't do certain things because I'm afraid I'll die if I do.

"And beside all of that, I'm only doing any of it because I wanted to prove to you that I could be better, and that I could deserve for you to love me again. If you think that any of this has been easy for me, or that I've moved on, then you're wrong. I've only been doing it for you."

"So then why the hell didn't you answer the

phone?" he shouted, slamming his fist into the back of the sofa. "If you've been so desperate to talk to me, why give up your first chance?"

"I already told you," I shot back. "I thought you had moved on, and I thought if I picked up that phone, you'd just confirm it. I didn't know you were in a car accident. I couldn't have known, and if I did I would have been at the hospital. But I was *finally* feeling happy and learning how to be that way on my own. I was having a good night, and I didn't want to ruin that by hearing that you were done with me – that everything I'd been working so hard for was out of reach. But none of that even matters, Adam, because it wasn't you on the other end."

"It matters to me, Mark" he yelled, tears forming in his eyes. "While you've been getting better and better, my life has been falling apart."

"What are you talking about, Adam? What's going on with you?" I asked in a softer tone, reaching out to touch his shoulder. He pulled away sharply.

"I got suspended last night. I don't have a job for the rest of the semester. And Aaron was my only friend and he's probably never going to speak to me again after this accident. Now it turns out I can't even count on you," he said, his voice breaking.

"Adam, what happened?" I asked. "Why did you get suspended? How did you get into an accident? Were you drinking?" That must have been the exact wrong question to ask. His face contorted into an angry display I'd never seen before, as if I'd pushed an actual button that set him off.

"You happened Mark. You are what happened to me," he said pointedly.

He's right. You ruined his life.

"Adam, you don't mean that. You're upset, I get that. But this," I said, gesturing at his arm. "None of this is my fault."

"Of course it is, Mark," he screamed. "Everything was fine last year! We were doing so well. We were going to start our family and have everything we ever wanted, but you ruined it."

Yep, right again. That was all you.

"I didn't mean to ruin anything," I said, tears welling up in my eyes. "You have to know that, Adam.

When we went to L.A., I did the best that I could. I've been doing the best that I could this entire time."

"Well, it wasn't enough, was it?" he shouted. "You couldn't just hide your grief for a few days, and we lost everything. And don't forget that you lied to me about wanting kids in the first place."

Look at him, you did this to him. I was overcome with guilt. Maybe he was right, maybe it was all my fault.

"Of course I wanted to have children with you Adam. I was just hurting. I said I didn't because I was afraid I'd mess it up again. I lost my dad, Adam," I said, openly crying. "My only family. How was I supposed to just move on?"

"Your only family? What about me, Mark? What about our baby?" he said, now crying as well, but still visibly angry.

"That's not what I meant. It was just him and me until I met you. I didn't grow up with a big family like yours. And you want to talk about losing everything? I lost you and him at the same time," I said.

"What are you talking about, Mark?" he asked,

his voice dripping with disdain. "I've only been gone a few months."

"No, Adam. You might have only moved out a few months ago, but I lost you the second we came home from L.A. without a baby," I said, tears now covering my face running down onto my neck. "You never forgave me for what happened with the baby. And I get it. I do. I know how badly you wanted to have a child. But he wasn't even our baby yet. We'd only even known about him for a few weeks. But regardless of any of that, you were still supposed to be my husband. 'In sickness and in health' right? You were supposed to stay by my side and help me heal. But it was like I was reaching out to you and my hands were passing right through, because you weren't really there. You'd checked out on me.

"You feel like you were just my babysitter? It's because that's who you chose to be. Life got a little hard and it was your turn to take care of me for a change, and you bailed! You can't just say you'll be there for somebody and call it good. You have to actually show up, Adam."

"Don't you dare talk to me about bailing, Mark," he said, stepping up so close to me that I could smell the liquor on his breath again. "You completely gave up. You quit your job and I was the one who had to take over our finances and make sure we didn't go broke without your income. I had to make sure you ate, and bathed, and drive you to your appointments after you stopped driving."

"Oh poor you," I shouted through tears. "You had to be an adult and a husband. If you'd gone into those appointments with me like I *begged* you to, you'd know how hard I was fighting just to hold on to the tiny shred of sanity I had left because we were still trying to find medication that worked for me. You'd know that I didn't eat because even though I knew we had plenty of savings to last us *years,* you were so worried about money that I didn't want to add any expenses. I didn't bathe some days because I was sure that something in the water would poison me. You'd know how many days you went to work and I sat in the closet terrified that something or someone would come and kill me, and considering just killing myself to end the suffering

- mine and yours."

I could tell he wanted to interrupt me but I didn't let him, despite the fact that I was now crying even harder and barely able to speak. "You'd know that losing my dad broke my heart, and that you broke it a little bit more every day with the annoyed way you looked at me, and the way you only gave me compulsory goodbye kisses, and then later stopped showing me any affection at all. And you'd know that I spent the last of those appointments that I went to explaining to the therapist that I wouldn't be returning because I couldn't bear to burden you with having to drive me anymore, because I'd overheard you tell someone on the phone that you wished I'd just get over it so you could have your life back."

He stepped back, shaking his head. "How was I supposed to show you any affection, or be happy about taking care of you when all I could think about was how we'd lost our baby because of you? You're right, maybe I didn't ever forgive you. But how could I? You knew how important that was to me and you fucked it up. Maybe I did shut down emotionally toward you, but

I stayed. I stayed until you were suffocating me so badly that I couldn't stand it anymore, because you weren't the man I fell in love with. You were just an empty, worthless shell."

There it is. Worthless. Just like you thought. Can't hide from it now.

I couldn't speak. I couldn't move. That last sentence echoed in my ears as if time had frozen on it. I might have just stood there forever if Grayson hadn't come down the stairs.

"I think it's time for you to go," I heard him say from over my shoulder. I still felt like I was frozen in a haze, no choice but to let him take over.

"Fuck you. Why don't you leave? This is my house," Adam said. I might have felt like I deserved what he'd been saying to me, but Grayson didn't. That brought me back to my senses.

"No, it's not. You walked out on me once," I said angrily. "Do it again. And use the door, I'd prefer for the rest of my windows to stay intact."

"Fine. I'm filing the divorce papers today," Adam said, stomping toward the door.

"Sure you'll be sober enough? Seems like you picked up your dad's old habit," I said. I immediately hated myself for being so mean, but the words were already gone.

"Go to hell, Mark," he said as he walked out, slamming the door behind him. I felt like I was already there.

"Are you okay?" Grayson asked. "I'm sorry. I really tried not to get in the middle, but he went too far."

"Thank you," was all I could manage. Grayson wrapped his arms around me and held me tight. I cried for what felt like hours before I finally pulled away.

"We should get to work," I said, wiping my face, still trying to calm down.

"Hey, forget it," Grayson said softly. "I'm the owner, remember? I think I just decided we're closed today."

"I can't let you do that," I said.

"Too late," he said, tapping away at his phone. "I already told all of the other employees to take the day off, paid. I'll run and leave a sign on the door in a little while. But for now, let's get you taken care of. Come on." He led me over to the sofa to lie down.

"I'm gonna go let Dolly out and get your medications and some tea. I'll be right back, okay? I'm not gonna leave you, I promise."

He must have known that my mind was already running wild. Adam had delivered the perfect crushing blow, whether he'd meant to or not. And I knew that no matter what happened after that, our relationship was over. We'd both dealt blows that could never be healed enough to allow a real love to flourish again.

Worthless. That's all you are. All you've ever been. All you'll ever be. Grayson will see that soon and he'll leave just like everyone else in your life ever has. You have nothing to offer to anyone. They'd all be better off if you were dead. Especially Adam.

I couldn't stop picturing a funeral devoid of anyone in attendance – every chair empty, with me in the coffin as the only one in the room. Then a grave stone reading, "Here lies Mark Diaz, worthless nobody."

I finally snapped out of it when Dolly started

gently licking the tears off of my face. I sat up and picked her up into my lap and she laid her head on my shoulder like she was hugging me. Even she seemed to understand how terribly sad I was.

Grayson brought in a tray with tea for the both of us in addition to my medications and a small bowl of dog food left over from the night before for Dolly. I took my pills and tried to drink the tea but I couldn't calm down enough. Grayson pulled me close and I lay in his lap and cried myself to sleep.

When I woke up, Grayson was still sitting with my head resting on his legs. Dolly was sitting on the other side of him and they were quietly watching TV together. As I began to stir, Grayson smiled down at me, his warm, compassionate gaze almost making me forget how broken I felt. Almost.

"Hey sleepyhead," he whispered as I sat up.

"Hey," I said groggily. "What are you still doing here?"

"I told you I wasn't gonna leave you, remember? I never break a promise."

"You're amazing, " I said, getting an even bigger

smile out of him. "I'm serious. How lucky am I to have had a panic attack in your diner's restroom? I know we haven't known each other very long but you honestly might be the best friend I've ever had."

He wrapped his arm around my shoulder, pulled me close to lie on his chest, and said, "same," then started flipping through the channels casually.

Strangely, even more than I felt terrible about everything that had happened with Adam, I predominately felt guilty for dragging Grayson into it and for feeling so bad while he was there with me. I hadn't realized how important he had become to me until then. Somehow, his feelings had come to be more important to me than my own.

"I love you, you know that?" Grayson whispered, pulling me back out of my thoughts. He must have felt my body tense in reaction and continued, "I mean, not like I'm *in* love with you. Just...you mean a lot to me, and I'm here for you - whether you want to work it out with Adam or not."

I swallowed hard, fighting back tears. It had been so long since anyone had shown genuine care for me. It meant more to me than I could ever hope to express to him. Not only that he cared for me, but that he did it while seemingly wanting and needing nothing from me.

Unconditional love seems like such a simple thing to ask of the world. Yet it remains such an elusive luxury that it is almost overwhelming when in rare moments it reveals itself to us in its purest form – when we've hit our darkest depths and it reaches in and illuminates. It took everything in me not to openly start crying again as I whispered a simple reply, "same."

I felt his chest rise slightly with a small chuckle; and then we sat in silence. He didn't pull away, or even look at me. He just held onto me tightly, like he knew as well as I did that he was the only glue keeping me together. We stayed that way until he needed to go get more food for Dolly.

When he returned from his house, he brought two bags with him – one for him and one for Dolly – so that he could spend the night and make sure I made it through the night okay. I tried to assert that I'd be fine on my own. In the end, he had to calm me down several times throughout the day, as Adam's biting words replayed in my mind and almost sent me spiraling.

So he stayed. He started the night out on the sofa, but after a particularly graphic mental obsession with killing myself left me sobbing into my pillow, he moved upstairs into the bed with me. Again, he pulled me close and held me with such innocence and compassion that it left me awestruck.

I began to cry harder not because I was sad, but because I felt so fortunate to exist in that singularly magic instant where I had become so aware of the great light that had entered my life. I had lived in darkness for so long, my heart and spirit so weary and lifeless that I felt as if they might atrophy. Yet here was this kindred soul who had found me at the exact moment I needed him most, as if whatever gods were in charge of the universe had finally smiled upon me and sent him to rescue me.

I slept the most peaceful sleep I had in over a year that night, with Grayson on one side of me, holding me to keep me grounded, and Dolly on the other, her tiny head resting on my legs. I couldn't bring myself to say it to him, but I'm fairly certain he saved my life that night. I don't know how I would have survived the storm rampaging through my mind on my own.

The next morning, we went back to work and for a few days it seemed as if everything might go back to normal. Well, the new version of normal I'd grown accustomed to, at least. But life's never quite that black and white, is it? As November wore on and the trees shed their leaves with a renewed vigor, there were many days where I couldn't bring myself to leave my house. I did my best to control my depression and OCD. I kept attending virtual therapy with Dr. Rodriguez, and she increased my medication slightly to try to help. But there were several days where I simply wasn't strong enough.

Midway through November the time came for the in-person appointments that Dr. Rodriguez had planned. Grayson drove me to the first two. For the third, on the day before Thanksgiving, I drove myself to the appointment that I was originally supposed to bring Adam to. I was determined not to let the entire month go by without making some kind of progress. If that progress couldn't be with Adam, then I owed it to myself to make progress with myself, *for* myself.

"So, things didn't exactly go as we'd hoped this month," Dr. Rodriguez said as the hour began to drawn near to its end, after we'd discussed the previous week's events.

"Definitely not," I said with a small laugh. "But I drove here today. I know that sounds like a simple task, but it feels like a big victory for me. I feel like every month I've made at least one big step toward getting my old life back. It feels good."

"I'm glad to hear that," she said with a warm smile. "But when you say your old life, does that still mean you're hoping for reconciliation with your husband?"

"Yes and no," I said. "I mean, do I think we'll ride off into the sunset together and live happily ever after? Probably not. There's too much baggage there now, I think. I feel like that tie has been severed irrevocably. After that fight we had, I don't know how we could ever go back to being lovers. But I'd like to be his friend. As much negative energy as there is between us now, there was just as much, if not more, love there before. It's hard for me to imagine never speaking to him again."

"Have you tried to reach out to him?" she asked. "It's been almost a month. Perhaps enough time has passed that you've both had a chance to lick your wounds and come back to the table for a more civil postmortem on your relationship."

"No," I admitted. "Not because I don't want to. It's just – there's a lot of uncertainty there. He said he was going to send me divorce papers but I haven't received any. I guess I'm afraid that if I reach out, it'll be the final nail in the coffin. And I know that it's over. I truly do. I suppose there's just a tiny part of me that is still holding out hope."

"Well, you'll never know unless you ask," she said with a smile. "I know that doesn't sound like real advice, but in this situation it really is down to just ripping off the bandage, so to speak."

"I know. I'll try. After the holiday?" I suggested.

"A fair plan," she conceded. "In the meantime, what about this new guy – the scruffy, handsome one that drove you the last couple of times. The two of you seem close. Could that have anything to do with why you've accepted the end of your relationship with Adam? Are you possibly moving on *with* him?"

"Grayson? No, we're just friends," I insisted. "I mean, yes, we've grown very close. He's been a wonderful friend to me, so I guess in that way he is part of why I'm okay with letting go of Adam. But we're just friends, nothing more."

"I wouldn't be so sure about that," she said, cryptically glancing toward the window. "But, that's all we have time for today. I'll be out of town for the next week, so I'll see you the following Tuesday?"

I nodded, wondering how it was possible that she'd really just ended the session on such a confusing note. I began to understand what she might have meant as soon I walked outside. Grayson was sitting on the hood of my car, holding a balloon in a bright shade of green, my favorite color, and a small arrangement of flowers.

He was already a well-groomed man, but on this particular day he seemed to have put in extra effort. His beard was freshly trimmed, his hair combed perfectly. He was wearing a cleanly pressed dress shirt and blazer in place of his usual flannel shirt or t-shirt. He had a nervous energy about him that I'd never seen before.

"What are you doing here?" I asked. "Is that for me?"

"Well, I was just out for a walk and found these in a ditch and figured I'd pick them up. Then I realized I was right near here and thought I'd say hi," he said, a playful grin on his face. "Of course they're for you, you goof. I'm so proud of you for driving all the way here today." He handed me the flowers and balloon and wrapped his arms around me. Instead of just a regular embrace, however, this time he swept me off of my feet and spun me around.

"Grayson, thank you. You didn't have to do all of this," I said as he put me down. "How did you even get here?"

"I rode the bus. So, I'm gonna need a ride home if that's okay."

"Of course," I said, hugging him again. "I can't believe you did all of this. All I did was drive myself."

"But I know that it meant more than just that to you," he said. "Which means it meant more than just that to me, so really this celebration is 50 percent selfish."

"Okay, does that mean I only have to give you 50 percent of a ride home?" I joked.

"Well, I specifically took the bus so that I'd have an excuse for you to drive me. Besides, this is only 50 percent of the surprise. So I guess that depends on how badly you want to see the rest."

So, I drove him back to the cottage and he covered my eyes and walked me in. When he uncovered my eyes, I saw that he had set up an elaborate dinner. As I looked closer, tears filled my eyes and I recognized the food on the table – all from my father's recipes, the ones I'd held on to but never attempted to make.

"How... how did you," I stammered.

"I was looking for your brownie recipe the day that you fought with Adam because I wanted to cheer you up, and I found your dad's old recipe cards in the back of the box," he explained, taking my hands in his. "I hope it's okay that I copied them. I wanted to do something special for you when we got to this day, because this is it, you know?

"Maybe your situation with Adam isn't completely clear, and maybe you'll have more days here and there where you aren't strong enough to overcome every bit of your illnesses, and that's perfectly normal and okay. But driving was the last big hurdle. Now you can do everything you did before this all started. Sure, you need medication to be able to do it, but there's nothing wrong with that. You can have your life back, and I'm so incredibly happy for you, and proud of you for coming so far."

There was a split second while he was speaking where I involuntarily pictured the stove erupting and setting the entire cottage on fire. But my heart was so full of gratitude in the moment that quieting my mind was easy.

I couldn't muster any words, so I just pulled him close and held on until I could finally say, "Thank you,

Grayson. I don't have the slightest idea what to say to you right now beside that, but it doesn't feel like enough. You have been such an incredible friend to me, and I feel like I haven't done anything for you. I don't deserve all of this."

"I mean, you've basically doubled my baked good revenue since you took over for Chelsea," he said, laughing. "So if you just do some mental gymnastics, you can conclude that you paid for it yourself. But seriously, it's not about what you deserve. None of us deserve anything. But if we're lucky, the universe gives us people who loves us anyway. Now, enough of this mushy stuff. Let's eat before Dolly jumps on the table and beats us to it."

After dinner I stayed at his place for a bit, then headed home, feeling like I could handle anything. I was so grateful to Grayson for making me feel like I mattered – like it wasn't silly to see my baby steps as accomplishments. And he was right, driving was my last big mountain to climb. There was nothing stopping me from taking my old life back.

I decided that Dr. Rodriguez was right about

reaching out to Adam, and I felt so good that I knew even if it went poorly, it wouldn't bring me down too far. So I dialed his number and held my breath. I didn't honestly expect him to answer, so when the line was picked up, I was a bit taken aback.

"Oh, hey," I said. "I didn't actually think you'd answer."

"Hey, Mark. It's Scotty," Adam's younger brother said in a hushed tone. He was being surprisingly pleasant – Adam's family had never liked the fact that he married another man and the few times I'd interacted with them had been tense. "Adam's not exactly in a good place right now, bud. Maybe when we get him sorted out I can tell him to give you a call?"

"Oh, Scotty, hey. What's wrong with him? Is there anything I can do?" I asked, trying not to panic.

"I don't think so, man. Look, he asked us not to say anything to you, but I feel like I owe you at least this – he's been drinking... a lot. But Momma's got a plan to take him to an AA meeting on Friday." he said. "Not sure there's much of anything anyone can do for him other than that, but we're trying. I gotta go, but I'll have him call you, I promise."

The line went dead and I let myself fall back onto the bed. I'd been worried about Adam drinking the day I'd seen him. I was kicking myself for not trying to help him. But I decided that there was nothing I could do that night. If he specifically asked his family not to contact me, then he didn't want my help, and I knew they'd take care of him. Whether or not they'd liked me, I'd always known at least his mother loved him. She would make sure he got the help he needed.

Grayson called after that and invited me to have, as he called it, "Day After Thanksgiving-Thanksgiving Dinner" with his parents, Roy and Donna. So on Thursday, Grayson opened the diner as a buffet for homeless people to go and eat a Thanksgiving meal. I volunteered to help him and realized that it was becoming increasingly difficult not to be awestruck by his wonderful heart.

On Friday, I had insisted on making desserts in return for being invited into Roy and Donna's home for a holiday, and Grayson had spent the morning helping me. So, we drove over together. After Donna had let us in and introduced me to Roy, she nudged him and said, "They came together." Roy had given her a look as if she'd just spilled some ancient family secret. I glanced at Grayson and he was giving them both the same look.

Donna had the same kind eyes as Grayson. The rest of his facial features had clearly come from Roy, who looked almost exactly like Grayson, but with gray hair and a few wrinkles. Their home reminded me a lot of Grayson's, with their own set of mismatched furniture and walls covered in family photos.

At the table after dinner, Donna said, "So Mark, Grayson has told us a lot about you."

"Oh really?" I asked. "At least a few good things I hope?"

"Oh, wonderful," Roy said, averting his eyes after Grayson shot him another of those looks. "I mean, he says you've been a great help at the diner. That Chelsea girl always struck me as a bit odd anyway. Don't you think, Donna?"

"Oh yes, she was very strange," Donna quickly agreed, clearly desperate to change the subject.

"How about I go get dessert then? You can tell me if my baking lives up to its reputation," I said, trying to give them an out.

I didn't bring it up through the rest of the time we were there, but I kept wondering what it was Donna and Roy were trying to keep secret. On top of the weird glances exchanged between the three of them, I kept catching whichever of Grayson's parents I wasn't directly talking to watching me with their face contorted as if they were fighting back tears.

As I drove us back to the diner to store the leftovers, Grayson broached the subject first. "Sorry Mom and Dad were being so weird," he said sheepishly. "They mean well."

"They're sweet," I said reassuringly. "I enjoyed getting to know them a bit. They really seem great."

He beamed at me, his large dimples revealing themselves again, and I left it at that until we were back at the diner.

"So," I said, hopping up to sit on the counter near where he was standing. "Do you want to tell me why they kept looking at me like I was dying? It's okay if you told them about... my situation. I'm not embarrassed about it anymore – mostly because of you."

"It's not that," he said, wringing a dish towel in his hands and looking at the floor. "I mean, they do know bits of that because I thought it would give them some comfort to know that someone who had struggled like Alex was making their way out of it. But, that's not what that was about."

"So, what was it?" I asked. "You know you can tell me anything, right?" He nodded, moving slowly closer. He inched closer until his face was so near mine that I could smell the gum he'd been chewing on his breath.

He looked right into my eyes and said, "I sort of told them that I've been falling for someone. I didn't tell them who, exactly, but I'm pretty sure they thought it was you."

I felt like the air had been knocked out of me and my lungs were vacuum sealed empty. I became acutely aware of how close he was standing and how quiet the room was as I asked, "Were they right?"

"I think you know the answer to that," he said, reaching for my hands.

Of course, I did. It may not have added up until that moment, but as he said it, all of the signs flashed at me like the skyline of the Vegas strip. The tender way he held me when I was upset. The way he smiled from ear to ear and laughed even when I knew my jokes weren't funny. The way he'd celebrated even my smallest victories. The "I love you," that I'd taken as platonic. *"How did I miss this? Did I miss this? Or did I just not want to admit seeing it?"* I thought to myself. But there was no time to think that train through, because he was speaking again, and I couldn't risk missing it.

"Look, I know it's not right, Mark," he said, "You're still married and you just got to a really great place. And I know that you can't possibly feel the same way about me. I know it's selfish of me to even be telling you this. But I'm falling for you so hard, and I can't hold it in any longer because keeping it from you is eating me up. I've never felt like this before."

I hated seeing him so torn up. I couldn't even

process my own feelings about what he was saying because I so badly just wanted to comfort him. "Grayson," I said softly as I pushed a strand of his long hair that had fallen in his face back into its place. I should have realized I'd opened the door for what happened next.

He looked up at me slowly, then gradually drew closer and finally pressed his lips against mine. His lips were soft, his breath sweet. Even on his day off, he still smelled like coffee mixed with his cologne. His beard scratched against my face, which normally would have bothered me, but felt nice in this case.

My first instinct was to push him away. But I knew exactly how I felt. The timing was wrong, I couldn't deny that. But I also couldn't deny that I was falling for him just as much as he was for me. I wrapped my arms around his back, pulled him close, and kissed him back.

Chapter Seven | *Adam*

I slammed the door to what had evidently become only Mark's house behind me. I was so blindly angry that I didn't even consider how I was going to get home. I wasn't going to just sit around and watch Mark and his new whatever. I ordered a car from an app and walked to the nearby park to wait for it to pick me up.

I couldn't believe that Mark had actually had the audacity to say the things he'd said to me. When I got home, I almost got in my car and drove to the jail to check on Aaron, but I was angry at him too. I'd put my trust in him, and he'd lied to my face about that phone call. I went upstairs and threw back four shots of whiskey.

That only made me angrier. I kept thinking about everything Mark had said to me and ended up slamming my fist through the kitchen wall. The worst part was that I felt nothing in response to it – no guilt, no shock at what I'd done, nothing. I opened the bottle again and drank until I passed out.

Late in the afternoon, I was awakened by loud banging on my front door. I lay perfectly still, hoping whatever fresh hell it might be would just leave me alone.

"I know you're in there, dude. Open the fucking door," Aaron's muffled voice called through the door. I weighed my options as well as I could in my buzzed state. I could open the door and have my second ugly confrontation of the day, or I could keep hoping he'd just give up and go away. The latter didn't seem likely, so I begrudgingly opened the door.

"Hey," I said curtly.

"Really dude? 'Hey'? That's all you have to say to me?" he asked angrily.

"What would you like for me to say Aaron?" I asked.

"Oh, I don't know man. How about 'sorry I dragged you into my bullshit drinking problem and got you a fucking DUI'?" he said in a mocking tone.

"Yeah, because I put a gun to your head and made you drive the car," I said sarcastically. "Grow up and take responsibility for your own choices. Like, for example how you didn't tell me my husband called me, and apparently deleted the call from my phone since I never saw it in the call logs? Yeah, I saw Mark today. Did you really think I'd never find out?"

"You've gotta be shitting me bro," he said with a scoff. "Yeah, I protected your sorry ass from that call because I knew it'd fuck you up even worse than you already were. Sue me. And you're the king of avoiding responsibility. That's basically your entire existence."

"What is that supposed to mean?" I demanded.

"You sit around whining all day about your sad, desperate divorce like it wasn't your own goddamn choice. You bitch about your husband like he just went to the store one day and bought a lifetime subscription of depression and whatever other shit you decided was too much for you to handle. You're like a fucking hurricane dude. You just blow through people like they aren't even there and then you move on and leave them to clean up your mess. Were you even going to bother checking on me at all? It's been over 12 hours!"

"No, actually, I wasn't," I admitted, raising my voice and stepping up nearer to him. "I was pissed at you, and decided you could take care of yourself."

"Have you been drinking? Are you fucking serious? We were just in a wreck because we were drinking! You know what, man? I feel sorry for you," he said, recoiling at my breath and starting to gather up his things around the room. "I'll pay whatever fines I have to and I'll get my life back together and move on. But unless you get some serious help, all you're ever going to be is a pathetic drunk."

He slammed the door behind him before I had a chance to respond. For the second time in less than 24 hours I was left feeling like I'd just been attacked and left to the wolves. I reached for the bottle of whiskey and found that I'd finished it before I'd fallen asleep. I rummaged through my cabinets and found nothing else to drink.

Desperate for something to take the edge off, I walked down to Sofia's. It was only 2pm, so I expected that Aaron wouldn't be there for a few hours. But he must have stopped by there before he'd gone to my apartment, because Sofia scrambled around the bar to meet me as soon as I walked in.

"You can't drink here no more, *Mijo*," she said. "You've got a problem and you need to get some help."

"Sofia, not you too," I said. "Look, I don't have a problem. I'm just going through a rough time right now is all."

"Do you know how many times I've heard that one, blue eyes?" she asked, taking my face in her tiny hands. "I know you don't wanna admit it to yourself, but you do have a problem. I'm sorry I didn't see it sooner. And I like you too much to watch you drink yourself to death. So, you go and get sober. And after that if you wanna come in here and get some food, it's on me. But you can't drink here no more, you hear me?"

I didn't even bother answering her. I turned and stormed out without a single word. I took a cab to an upscale bar across town and settled in for a long night. About $100 in, someone bumped my arm and my drink spilled across my lap.

"Watch where you're going, asshole," I slurred. I felt a strong grip on my arm. I was spun so quickly that I didn't see who had done it until after a punch to the face landed me flat on the floor. I looked up and saw a man roughly the same size as me, but more muscular, standing over me. His punch shouldn't have blown me over so easily. I must have been drunker than I'd thought.

"How 'bout you watch your mouth before I break your other arm, idiot?" he asked.

I should have kept my mouth shut, or just gotten up and walked away. Instead, I said, "Is that all you got, tough guy?"

It wasn't. He kicked me in the ribs, then again. Then he pulled me up by my shirt just to punch me in the face and knock me back down. My broken arm knocked up against the nearby stools a few times, but outright going for that arm seemed to be the line he wouldn't cross. Other than that, he kicked and punched me anywhere he could reach. The whole time, I could hear laughing, and I wondered what kind of jerk would just be laughing at someone who was getting beaten up.

Then I caught my reflection in the metal siding of the bar and realized it was me. He kept going because *I* was laughing.

"You think it's funny you son of a bitch?" he yelled as he delivered another kick to my side. I laughed even harder, still unsure why. It definitely wasn't a reaction to humor. It wasn't even my normal laugh. It was a visceral, almost feral sound, like each blow he delivered was causing my body to release some kind of demonic energy bit by bit.

I didn't make any effort to stop him. I didn't even ask for help. I just lay there, letting him kick me over and over until someone finally stopped him and kicked us both out.

I took a cab home and then stood in front of the long bathroom mirror, examining my naked body. Large purple and blue bruises were already forming all over. I stared at the bruises for a long while, wondering how my life had taken such a dramatic turn. A couple of years earlier all I'd wanted was to teach English and start a family with my husband. Now I was staring at two sets of bruises, unsure which incident any of them even came from. I'd fallen so hard I didn't know how I could possibly get back up.

I went to bed for lack of anything better to do, and stayed there until after noon the following day. I left the house that day only because I was out of liquor. I stocked up at the nearest store with as much as I could carry. Then I stayed holed up in my apartment for a week. One week turned into two, turned into three. Just me and a bottle. All day. Every day. I left the apartment only a handful of times. Once to pick up the divorce papers I intended to send to Mark, and the rest were to buy more liquor.

As Thanksgiving neared, I began to feel even more lonely. Mark and I usually spent the holidays with his father. After he died, we spent the following Thanksgiving alone at our house. We didn't even cook anything special. Mark was in an even worse funk than usual and had locked himself up in the bathroom all day. So I spent the day checking in on him occasionally. I had a feeling that this one, all by myself, was going to feel even worse than that.

But on the Monday before the holiday, I

received a surprise call from my youngest brother, Scotty. He was only 22 and still lived at home with our mother while he went to college. It was six in the morning and I was severely hung-over, so I wasn't exactly a shining example of a big brother when I answered.

"Hey bubba, it's Scotty," he said in his thick southern accent when I answered.

"I know it's you Scotty. I have caller ID."

"Oh... Well, I never hear from you. Didn't know if you had my number," he said, sounding like he really thought that made sense.

"I don't ever hear from you either, Scotty," I replied curtly. "Do you need something?"

"I... no," he said, sounding disappointed.

"Scotty, what?" I insisted.

"I, um, I just wanted to see if you'd come for Thanksgiving this year," he whispered. "Mark can come too. Everybody will be real nice. I promise."

"You want me to come for Thanksgiving?" I asked incredulously. "And you wanted to ask me that at 6:01 am? Is this a prank?"

"Oh shoot," he said. "I'm sorry Adam, I forgot about the time difference."

Scotty and I had never been particularly close. There were 15 years between us in age, so we'd mostly grown up separately. He, like the rest of my brothers and our parents, had been very vocally against me marrying Mark. I tried not to hold it against him, because he was young, but we never really bonded. I cared about him, but I never felt close to him or like I particularly liked him. But I'd never heard him sound as sad as he did on the phone. I suppose whatever shred of empathy my binge drinking hadn't washed away kicked in.

"No, don't be sorry. It's okay," I said with a sigh. "*I'm* sorry. I just... had a long night. That's all. Look, are you absolutely sure you want me to come?"

"I'm sure. I swear," he said, his voice returning to normal.

"Then I guess I'll see you in a couple of days," I said and hung up.

I spent the day packing, deciding I'd take enough to last me through Christmas if things went well. Not having a job makes it pretty easy to keep your travel dates flexible. I was a bit nervous that Mark would block my credit cards and I wouldn't be able to get a flight. But I should have known that that's not who he is.

I flew in on Wednesday and, on my way through the airport, caught a glimpse of my reflection. Saying I looked like complete ass would be too kind. Aside from my clean clothes, I looked like I had been living on the street. Scotty was supposed to pick me up at the airport, and I couldn't let him see me that way. I was already dreading having to explain the divorce and my still broken arm to my family. The last thing I needed was to have to tell them about getting my ass kicked in a bar. My other brothers, the twins Drew and Mitch, would never let me live that down.

I bought some very overpriced toiletries and makeup in the gift shop and ducked into the bathroom. I did my best with one arm to cover up the visible bruises that remained, shaved, and fixed my hair. I stared at myself for a moment and realized just how different I looked. I'd lost weight, presumably from replacing several of my meals over the last month with liquor. My eyes had dark bags under them that even the makeup did little to conceal. My hair had grown longer than I'd ever had it before and even after styling it, it was a mess. But I knew that this would have to do.

I made my way outside and found Scotty waiting in a small, beat up, early-90s Toyota. I hadn't seen him in a few years, and was surprised to find that as he matured he was starting to look like me - at least, how I'd looked before all of the mess I'd gotten myself into. He had the same slightly crooked nose structure, the same square jaw. Even his hair, which had been much lighter before, had darkened to almost match mine. As we drove the 15 miles from the city to our tiny hometown, I asked him cursory questions about school and his life. When he asked, I explained that my broken arm had come from a car accident with as few details as possible.

He had a nervous energy about him for the entire drive that was making me feel almost as carsick as his erratic driving. I tried to put it out of my mind and just focus on the road. But the empty West Texas skyline didn't offer much in the way of distraction.

When we finally arrived at my mother's house, I was surprised to see that there were no other cars.

"Are Drew and Mitch driving in tomorrow?" I asked.

"They aren't coming this year," he said, after a long pause.

"Oh. It's not because of me, is it? Because I don't mind going to a hotel. I don't want to intrude on whatever you guys normally do," I offered.

"No... no. It's not because of you," he said, a solemn look coming over his face. "It's because of me, and a little because of Momma. But mostly me."

"Oh," I said, unsure what else to say. My brothers had always been very close to my mother. I couldn't imagine what would make them miss Thanksgiving with her. "Is everything okay?"

He took a breath, started to speak, then stopped. I felt bad for him, but he was also making me intensely nervous, which was making me crave a hard drink.

"Hey, look," I said. "I know we're not close. But we're still brothers. You can talk to me. Or don't. Either way, it's up to you. But I am a lot older than you. So chances are I've got some life experience that might help me help you."

"That's sort of the problem," he said, looking at me directly for the first time since we left the airport. Then, very rapidly, almost in a panic, he blurted, "I came out to Momma and the boys at my birthday party last month; and I'm so sorry for the things I said when you got married. I was just a stupid kid and I didn't know any better. Anyway both of the boys got mad and they haven't talked to me since then. And they got into a huge fight with Momma when she tried to talk to them about it and now it's probably her last Thanksgiving and they aren't coming and-"

"Whoa, whoa, Scotty, slow down" I said, trying to process all of the information he'd just dumped on me and decide which shocking revelation to cover first. "I definitely want to come back to you coming out. But first, what do mean when you say it's probably Momma's last Thanksgiving?"

"Oh, crap. I wasn't supposed to say anything. She wanted to tell you herself," he said, a terrified look spreading across his face. He looked conflicted. He clearly wanted to tell me, but felt like he couldn't. I put my hand on his arm to try to reassure him. "Momma's got cancer, Adam. It's bad. They gave her six months and it's already been four."

I sat back, stunned. It had been a long time since I'd been home, and even longer since I had a good relationship with my mother. But I'd always thought we had time to fix our relationship if we wanted to.

"Is she inside?" I asked, holding my breath. He shook his head solemnly.

"She's in the hospital right now, recovering from pneumonia. Hoping she'll get discharged in the morning."

"Take me there, please," I said, my chest tightening. He drove me toward the hospital in complete silence. I wanted to talk to him about his own issues, but my head was spinning. "Wait," I said, noticing a bar. "Stop here first."

Scotty eyed me dubiously as he pulled into the bar's parking lot. I invited him in with me and he reluctantly followed.

"I don't really drink, Adam," he said sheepishly.
"I read a study at school that says you can be
genetically predisposed to alcoholism and, well, you
obviously remember Dad."

"That's bullshit," I said. "I have a drink every
once in a while and I'm fine."

He eyed the cast on my arm as if he knew I was
lying, sighed, and sat at the bar next to me while I
ordered. One drink quickly turned into many, until I felt
buzzed enough to handle what was coming. As I drank
shot after shot of tequila, and he nursed a single soda,
we discussed his coming out.

"I'm really sorry I wasn't supportive when you
married Mark," he said. "I think I already sort of knew
that I was – am – gay too, and I was so ashamed of
myself. But it was easier to take it out on you."

"Well, Scotty, I hope you know now that there's
nothing to be ashamed of," I said, my words already
beginning to slur. "And for what it's worth, I forgive
you. You were just a kid. Drew and Mitch, on the other
hand, are assholes. And I'm sorry they treated you the
same way they treated me." I drank another shot, numb

to the burn on my throat at that point. "But I've been through all of this before. So if you need advice or anything, I'm here. I'll tell you one thing's for sure. You're lucky Dad is dead. He was the worst part for me."

He seemed hurt by that last bit, and I might have felt bad for that if I had been able to feel anything. I paid our tab and we finally headed to the hospital.

As we entered, I felt like the hallways were closing in on me. Every noise sounded like it was being funneled through ear muffs. I looked over at Scotty and saw that he looked scared. Instinctively, I offered him my hand and he took it. Like a zombie, I walked what felt like miles down the small corridor until we finally reached my mother's room.

Scotty entered slowly and quietly, but I remained at the doorway. Hattie King had always been known around town as a strong woman. She'd had to be. When my father was at his most drunk, he'd beat her badly. When we were old enough to try to defend her, he'd beat me and my brothers too. But she always got the worst of it and kept carrying on.

But lying there in that hospital bed, she was almost unrecognizable. Normally a robust woman, she looked thin and frail. Her trademark blonde hair was gone, replaced with a scarf wrapped around her bald head. I felt like I was frozen to the ground. No matter how much I told my feet to move, they wouldn't carry me forward.

"You gonna stand there all day or are you gonna come give your momma a hug?" she asked, surprising me. She'd appeared to be sleeping until then. I finally stumbled toward her bed and leaned in to hug her. "Oh baby, it is good to see you, but you smell like a distillery."

"Sorry," I whispered. "Are you... How are you feeling?"

"Well, I've been better, but I've been worse," she said with a weak smile. "But what on earth happened to you?" She rubbed the cast on my arm, shaking her head.

"Let's just say it's been a rough few months," I said, trying to dodge the subject.

"Scotty, how much did your brother here have

to drink before you brought him here?" she asked, raising an eyebrow at me.

Scotty looked down at his feet and hesitated. I could tell he was trying to talk himself out of selling me out. But he still said, "A lot."

"Mmhmm," she said suspiciously. "And how long have you been drinking this way?" she asked, turning her attention back to me.

"I don't know," I lied. "I just have a drink here and there to take the edge off. What's the big deal?"

"I think you know damned well what the big deal is," she said, raising her voice. That seemed to strain her, as she then erupted into a long coughing fit. Scotty rushed to her side and helped her sit up into a more comfortable position.

"I didn't come here to talk about me," I said. "Scotty told me, Momma. I know you're... dying." It was difficult to get that last word out. My mouth fought me hard on forming it.

"Well, I'm still gonna be dyin' tomorrow, son," she said. "You, though, are gonna sit your little butt down and tell me what's been going on with you."

I sat on the edge of the bed and tried to come up with an explanation that made me feel better. But at a certain point, lying to everyone including yourself wears on your soul. I was undeniably exhausted of pretending to be fine. So, I told the truth – about Mark and the divorce, about my job, about Aaron and the accident. Most importantly, I told her about the drinking, and finally admitted to myself that it was a problem. I felt like a weight had been taken away. But a scary amount of uncertainty at how I would fix it replaced it.

"Listen to me, boy," she said sternly as she clutched my knee when I was done. "I know you remember how much of a son of a bitch your daddy turned into when he was drinking like this. I still wish to God every day that I could go back in time and find a way to get us away from him without worrying that he'd find us and kill us all. Now I know you don't have that kind of hate in your heart, but I don't want to see you throw your life away the way your daddy did. You had a good career and a good man. Don't you want that back?"

She laid her head back as she began coughing again. I knew I wanted my career back. There was no question about that. But I had no idea if I wanted to try to win Mark back, or if I even had a chance with him again after everything that had happened. I didn't answer.

"There's an AA meeting at the Methodist church every Friday morning," she said when she caught her breath. "We're going this week. All three of us, as a family. Your brother and I will help you through this."

Scotty smiled a full smile at me for the first time since I'd arrived, and my mother squeezed my hand tight. I agreed to try AA on the condition that no one say anything about it to Mark. Things were too uncertain between us for me to drag him into it.

We sat with her for a couple of hours until she fell asleep, then I went back to the house with Scotty. He stayed awake to prepare parts of the next day's meal, but I crashed on the couch as soon as we were settled.

The morning of Thanksgiving, we got a call that our mother could come home. So we picked her up and helped her get settled at the house. I helped Scotty make the meal and had a surprisingly fun time bonding with him. I had to admit it was nice to finally feel like I actually had a real brother.

I had such a nice time, in fact, that I almost didn't crave a drink. Almost. By the time we finished, I couldn't stop thinking about it. I wasn't proud of it, but I rummaged through the kitchen in search of any alcohol. All I found was an old bottle of cooking wine. I didn't even care what it was. I drank most of it, then ate little bits of leftovers to try to mask the smell on my breath. That managed to get me through the rest of the night.

The next morning though, I woke up with an even more intense craving. I went to the kitchen looking for the rest of the cooking wine, but found the bottle sitting empty by the sink.

"You're not as sneaky as you think," Scotty said, suddenly entering the room behind me with his arms crossed. Without a car of my own there, I was left with no choice but to try to ignore the craving. Much easier said than done. I kept thinking about the sweet burn and merciful numbness that alcohol brings throughout the morning.

We ate breakfast in silence and then Scotty drove us all to the Methodist church across town. Despite being in a more worn down neighborhood, the building was well kept. The interior appeared to have been recently remodeled, except for the large basement room where the meeting we were attending was to be held.

There was a distinct dust smell that permeated the air as soon as the door was opened. Instead of the new carpet that covered the main floor, this room had stained old cement. There were plastic chairs lined in several rows in the center of the room and a few tables in the back that housed sad-looking refreshments.

I argued with my mother until she finally agreed to let us sit in the back. I was shocked by how crowded the room became as the meeting began. For such a small town, I hadn't expected such a large turnout.

We watched as the organizer of the meeting read off a few announcements, then the 12 steps of the program. Then, one by one, people began stepping to the front of the group and telling their stories. It was rough. Many of them mirrored my dilemma – excessive drinking triggered by some sort of personal life problem that had gotten far out of control.

But many of the stories were much worse, some even tragic. One woman told the group how she'd driven drunk with her infant in the car, got into an accident, and lost her baby. A young man who looked younger than Scotty detailed a car accident he had caused that killed an entire family in the car he hit. I cringed at the thought of how much worse my accident with Aaron could have been.

I was so shaken up that I raised slightly off of my chair and almost asked my family to leave with me. But I saw a familiar looking man approach the podium and sat back down.

Eric Jackson had aged quite a bit since we'd secretly dated in high school, but I still recognized him across a crowded room without a problem. His formerly jet black hair had begun to gray, and he was much stockier than the last time I had seen him. His wrinkled face showed signs of a difficult life, but he appeared to be in good spirits on this day.

"Hi everybody. My name is Eric, and I'm an

alcoholic," he said almost cheerfully. The group greeted him as they'd done everyone before him, and he continued. "So, I've been sober now for almost six months, and I feel great. But I gotta say, I almost stumbled last week. Some of you know I finalized my divorce recently. It was a lot harder than I expected. My wife -ex-wife- is still my best friend, I think. But she knew something about me that it's honestly taken all of my life to admit – I'm gay."

It was oddly cathartic for me to hear him say those words out loud. Eric had married his college girlfriend a few years after he and I broke up. I had wanted us to keep seeing each other after high school, but people around town were starting to whisper and Eric could never quite bring himself to admit his sexuality. Not that I could blame him. His father owned the biggest farm in town and his mother was on the city council. So the name Jackson carried a significant weight - one I could never hope to understand as the son of a known abusive alcoholic.

"Oh jeez," he continued. "I've never actually said those words to this many people before. That feels strange... but good. I think that's part of why I drank so much, you know? If I was drunk, I didn't have to face myself or the truth. Anyway, it wasn't fair for me to keep anchoring her down when I could never give her a full marriage. So I let her go.

"And now I am learning how to be a single gay father with an ex-wife. Let me tell you, that is no small task. But I'm learning that for the most part, no one is judging me as hard as I judge myself. So I'm trying to give myself a break. But, as I'm sure most of you know, it's not always easy. So, on this day after Thanksgiving, I just want to say that I'm really thankful for all of you. Thank you."

He moved back toward his seat and there was scattered applause from the group. As he walked back I saw him notice us and a small smile flashed across his face. I sat patiently through the rest of the speakers, then immediately went looking for him while my mother took Scotty and chatted with a few members of the group who she knew.

I stepped outside to see if I could find Eric heading toward his car, and then heard his familiar voice behind me. "Hey there, mister. Something I can help you find?"

"Hey," I said, much louder than I'd intended to, as I turned to face him. I reached out for a handshake, but he pulled me in for a big, awkward hug. "So, that was pretty impressive," I said, pulling away. "Never thought I'd hear you say those words."

"I know," he said, his face flushing. "And I owe you an apology for that. You gave me so much more in that relationship than I ever gave you. Same problem I had with Julie."

"Don't apologize," I said. "It would have been a lot harder for you to come out than it was for me. Not that it was easy, but I know it would have been worse for you. I always understood that. I've never held it against you. I promise."

"I know," he said, smiling. "That's what I loved about you. You always cared so much about me. You took care of me through all of that high school bullshit. But that doesn't mean I'm not sorry. Sometimes I think if I could just go back and change that one decision, my whole life would be different. But that kind of thinking is not really encouraged around here. Who knows though? Maybe I would have married you and we would have the kids by now."

My face burned and I was sure I had turned bright red. I reflexively tried to rub my wedding band, only to remember that I'd taken it off after my big fight with Mark after Halloween. "I don't think we'd be married," I said nervously. "We were so young."

"Maybe you're right. Still, it's a nice thought," he said with a shrug. "Hey do you have plans for dinner tonight? Maybe I can take you to one of the whopping two new restaurants this town has gotten in the past 20 years."

"I mean, how could I turn down such a glamorous offer?" I joked awkwardly. "Pick me up at seven?" He nodded and headed back into the church right as my mother and Scotty came out to meet me.

The three of us went for lunch and then home, where I spent the rest of the day nervously waiting for Eric to show up and fighting off the urge to go hunt down a drink. I tried helping Scotty proofread some term papers he was working on to distract myself. That didn't work. He was premed and I had a killer headache and couldn't focus on the unnecessarily large scientific words. So we tried playing video games. I was again surprised by how nice it was to feel like I had a brother who actually liked me for the first time since I'd come out to my family.

"Hey, Adam," he said late in the afternoon. "Do you think after Momma, um... Do you think after Momma's gone it would be okay if I moved out closer to you? I don't wanna be alone."

"You're not gonna be," I said without hesitation, putting my arm around him. "I'm staying as long as Momma needs me, and then you're coming home with me. I just need to find a bigger apartment."

"I never thought I'd see this day," my mother's voice called out behind us. She was walking slowly, clearly exhausted. I hurried to help her sit on the couch. "You two getting along so well, it's an answered prayer. I'll just have to keep praying that your other brothers come around."

By the time Eric showed up, my head was pounding incessantly and I felt like I was going to vomit any second. But he had seemed so hopeful at the meeting that I didn't want to let him down. So I ordered dinner for Scotty and our mother and set out with Eric to a small, dimly lit restaurant across town.

We reminisced about high school and all of the crazy things we'd done to keep our relationship a secret – like taking separate dates to prom, then faking sick and sneaking off outside to dance alone. We also commiserated over our failed marriages. I was doing my best to ignore my headache and nausea, but by the time we were finished with dinner, I felt like I could pass out at any second.

Eric excused himself to the bathroom, and I hurriedly went to the bar and ordered a shot of tequila, then another, then two more. Thinking I'd gotten away with it, I paid the bartender and headed back to our table, only to see Eric heading out the front door. I noticed a paper napkin with writing on it back at the table and went to read:

Adam,

It was nice catching up. Sorry I can't stay. Watching you take those shots was too tempting. I hope

*you'll keep going to meetings. Call me when you're
sober.*

*P.S. Sounds like you may have treated Mark the
way I treated you all those years ago. If you really love
him, don't make him do all the work. Fight for him. I
hope you get whatever it is you want.*

Eric

I felt like such an idiot. He'd left extra cash with
the note to pay for a cab, so I started to call one, kicking
myself for hurting him. That seemed to be my specialty,
hurting people I cared about. As I opened my phone to
call a cab, I noticed that Mark had called on Wednesday
while I was passed out. Scotty must have answered it
because it didn't read as a missed call.

I preoccupied myself with wondering what they
had talked about. Scotty had promised me that he
wouldn't say anything. But why would he answer the
phone and not say anything? But if he had told Mark
what was going on, and Mark hadn't called back, did
that mean he was officially over me? Did I deserve for
him to be over me anyway? Had I really neglected him
the way Eric was implying?

I gave up and walked right back up the bar. I stayed there until it closed, drinking so much that I didn't even remember how I got home when I woke up the next morning. I had a massive hangover, and only woke up because I felt a hard tapping on my shoulder. When I opened my eyes, there were three blurry figures standing above me.

It took a moment for my eyes to adjust. The light made my head throb as I tried to figure out who the third figure was since only Scotty and our mother had been there the night before. When my eyes finally adjusted, I was stunned to see the last person I'd ever expect to be teaming up with my family – Mark.

.

Chapter Eight | *Mark*

Kissing Grayson felt incredible, there was no way around admitting that. There was much more than a spark there. It was like wildfire. A kiss like that will make you believe in magic.

Then my phone rang. Scotty. I silenced it and it rang again. I reluctantly pulled away from Grayson.

Karma's coming for you for cheating on your husband. He's probably dead now, all because you couldn't keep your lips to yourself.

"Mark?" Scotty said in a hushed tone. "I know I said I wasn't supposed to call you, but I really don't think Adam can get through this without you. Can you come out here for a few days?"

I wanted so badly to hang up the phone and go back to kissing the beautifully kind man in front of me, instead of being pulled in to the mess waiting for me on the other end of the phone. But I owed it to Adam to help him one last time after everything we'd been through.

"I'll be there tomorrow."

"I get it," Grayson said, stepping away, having overheard Scotty's request.

"I promise you, I wouldn't even consider this if it wasn't an emergency," I said, reaching out for him.

"I know," he said smiling weakly but not accepting my hand. "He's still your husband. And you have a big heart, Mark. That's my favorite thing about you. So, go. I'll be here when you get back."

"You don't – I mean, I don't want you to feel like you have to wait for me, Grayson," I said, hopping off of the counter to move closer to him. "I can't give you an honest timeframe here. I hope that it'll only be a few days. But if it isn't, you should be free to move on with your life."

He stepped back toward me and placed a soft kiss on my forehead. "You're so strong, Mark. And you don't even realize it. I can be strong too. Go. Do what you need to do and, if you still want to, come back to me." He smiled his beautiful smile at me, hugged me tight, and then excused himself to the cottage. I finished up in the diner, hoping he'd come back. But he didn't and I didn't want to intrude on him so I headed home to pack.

But I hated to leave things the way we had. So the next morning on my way to the airport, I stopped by the cottage. He came to the door having just woken up, and for the first time, I could admit to myself how cute I thought he was in the morning. Right out of bed was the only time he ever let his hair be out of place, and it made the most of that time. It stuck out in every possible direction, giving him a frenzied look that was supremely endearing. He was wearing the glasses he only wore right before and after bed, and pajama pants with an oversized sweater.

"Good morning," he said, his dimples out in full force. I'd been worried that he would be upset with me or irritated that I'd awoken him. But there he was, smiling at me like a child smiles when they see their favorite friend.

"Good morning," I said, returning the smile.

Dolly came bursting through the front door. I picked her up and tried to balance her wiggling body in my arms. "Mind if I come in for a minute?"

"Of course not, you goof," he said, shaking his head. "Did I not make it very clear that I enjoy your company last night? Because I can try to make it clearer if I need to."

I laughed and stumbled inside with Dolly still in my arms. I sat on the sofa still holding her and she settled in my lap as I spoke. "So last night, you said that I could come back to you – if I still wanted to. And I couldn't leave without telling you that I do. I very much want to come back here and see where this goes."

"But Adam," he started.

"Has chosen to be my past," I interrupted. "He's very actively chosen that, and made it crystal clear that that's what he wants. And I've finally accepted that. Look, I have to do this, not because I want to be with him again, but because I need closure. The way he and I left things was volatile. But things weren't always that way between us, and I don't think I could ever give my whole heart to someone else if that's how it ends with him."

"So is that what you want? To give your heart to someone else, I mean?" he asked, clearly nervous. I carefully moved Dolly and stood to meet Grayson.

"I would very much like to try. And I would very much like that someone to be you," I said. "You mean so much to me. And that's why if we're going to do this, I want to do it right. And that means forgiving Adam and working for him to forgive me too."

"You're a good man, Mark Diaz. I hate that right now."

"Yeah, well my boss has set a really great example. Speaking of which, how much of a problem is it going to be for me to date my superior?"

"You know, I checked with the owner, and he told me it was cool. He also said I could have the morning off to drive you to the airport."

"Ah, I love that guy," I said, wrapping my arm around his waist as we walked toward the car.

"Yeah, I hear he's pretty fond of you too."

We drove to the airport mostly in silence. Dolly sat in the backseat, smiling with her head out the window. I laid my head on Grayson's shoulder and listened to him hum along with the radio. His voice was so soothing that I dozed off before we got there.

He woke me gently and we said goodbye in the parking lot so that Dolly wouldn't be left alone in the car. I wanted to kiss him so badly, but I knew it was better to wait until things were resolved with Adam.

I knew the flight would mess with my mind, so I took something to help me sleep and dreamed about what it would be like to be with Grayson when I returned.

Scotty picked me up at the airport and filled me in on everything I had missed. He was gay, his mother was dying, and Adam was an alcoholic. Big year at the King residence. He explained to me that a local bartender had called Hattie and informed her that Adam was blackout drunk and someone needed to pick him up. Scotty had brought him back to the house and dumped him on the couch.

That's where I found him. Even standing above, I could smell the alcohol radiating off of him. He looked even worse than the last time I had seen him.

Hattie, Scotty, and I were discussing how best to proceed when he woke up. He squinted up at me, confused. I saw the exact moment he realized it was me, because what little color had been left in his face vanished instantly.

He started to sit up quickly, looked nauseated, and laid his head back down. "Mark? What are you doing here?" he asked, closing his eyes again.

"I called him," Scotty said before I could say anything. "You need help bubba. Nobody can help you better than he can." I was surprised by how familiar they seemed with each other. It had been several years since they'd seen each other or even spoken on the phone. It was nice to see them getting along.

"Do you guys mind if I speak with Adam alone for a few minutes?" I asked. Hattie and Scotty left the room and I sat on the floor so that I could be as close to face to face as possible with Adam. "I'm sorry," I whispered to him.

He slowly opened his eyes again and craned his head to look at me disbelievingly. "*You're* sorry? I've basically been the world's worst asshole this year. I should be the one apologizing."

"I don't disagree. But I'm not spotless here either. We've both made mistakes. A lot of mistakes."

"Tell me about it," he said, sinking his head back onto the sofa. "I am sorry, for the record."

"I know you are," I said. I almost wished to myself that that was enough to repair what was broken between us. But I knew that it wasn't.

"I guess Scotty told you about the drinking?" he asked.

"More like he confirmed my suspicions," I admitted. He looked at me as if he didn't understand. "I mean, you came to the house smelling like a liquor store shelf turned over on you and threw a rock through my window."

"Right," he said, slapping a hand down over his eyes. "I'm sorry about that too. I'm sorry for all of it. Aaron told me I was like a hurricane. Maybe he was right."

"If he was, you'll always be my favorite hurricane," I tried to joke, squeezing his shoulder. "Sorry, you're not. I promise. And I owe you an apology too. I wasn't exactly kind to you that day either."

"But nothing you said was wrong," he said. "And I knew that. That's why it upset me so much. I think I've honestly known this whole time that I was being an asshole. It just took someone I knew a long time ago pointing it out to me to make me admit it to myself. You remember me telling you about Eric?" I nodded and he continued. "He was at the AA meeting Momma dragged me to, and we went to dinner to catch up last night. He sort of pointed out to me that I was treating you the same way that he treated me back in high school."

"How's that?" I asked.

"Like a support system, basically," he said, looking ashamed. "Like you were there to take care of me, but I wasn't as worried about *your* needs as I should have been."

"No, Adam," I started.

"No, it's true," he said, finally sitting up all the way. "If I'm ever going to kick this drinking habit, I've gotta face up to the truth. And the truth is that I was a really shitty husband to you when your dad died. I think part of it was because of my issues with my own dad. I couldn't understand how hard it was for you because when my dad died, I felt relieved. But your dad was always good to both of us. He treated me like his own son and I should have looked past my own issues to realize that and understand your loss.

"And with your mental illness, I felt like you were being weak – like if you just tried harder you could get over it. But I've been trying to quit drinking and I feel like I'm constantly fighting my own body. I feel like I have no power. And I know that that's how you felt, except it must have been worse for you because I did this to myself. And I'm so sorry, Mark."

I sat back against the sofa, processing everything he'd said. I had already forgiven him, I realized. But I also hated that it had taken him dealing with his own demons to try to look at my situation from my perspective.

It's not his fault you're a pathetic weakling. He was right about that in the first place. He's just trying to make you feel better now.

"*No,*" I thought, willing myself to replace the voice in my head with Grayson's telling me that I was strong. "*I'm not weak. I'm strong.*"

"I forgive you," I finally said to Adam as I moved to sit next to him on the sofa.

"Don't say that yet," he said, looking down at his feet. "I also need to apologize for accusing you of sleeping with your boss. Even if you were, I had no right to be upset about it. You were right. I was the one who walked out. And," he paused, his face contorting as if what he was about to say pained him. "I was sleeping with Aaron. I'm not anymore, but I was at the time. So I definitely had no right to accuse you of anything. I also, and I hate myself most of all for this, I slept with Wes."

It should have hurt me. But because I'd already suspected it and because I was starting to have feelings for Grayson, it rolled right off my back. In fact, I was mostly amused by the last bit. "Wait, Wes the Weasel?" I asked incredulously.

"Oh my god, I forgot about that nickname," he said burying his face in his hands. "I can't believe I cheated on you with someone we gave such a stupid nickname."

"At least he's good looking underneath that terrible personality," I said, playfully nudging him.

"Ugh, don't even get me started on his awful personality," he groaned. "He made my life hell afterward."

"Instant karma," I joked.

"I sincerely hope karma is not real, because I've got a lot worse coming if it is," he lay back down on the sofa, his head near my lap. My first instinct was to reach out and comfort him, but I thought better of it.

"I'm not sleeping with Grayson, by the way," I said. He looked relieved, but I didn't want to lead him on. "But we did kiss last night. It was the first time, I swear."

"So what are you doing here?" he asked, a hurt look crossing his face.

"I couldn't start something with him when you and I aren't finished. I owe you both more than that."

"I wouldn't say you owe me anything. I've been pretty terrible."

"Hey, I said I forgive you and I meant that. I came to help you because even if we aren't together anymore, I'll always care about you. And you are still legally my husband."

"Right," he said. He slowly stood and crossed into a nearby room. He returned with a folder containing a divorce agreement. "I had this drawn up. I just couldn't sober up long enough to sign and send it. Basically, we each keep what was ours before and split anything new. Except the house. You should keep it. Your hard work bought it. Of course we can change anything you don't agree to. I won't put up a fight."

"Adam, we can worry about this later. We need to get you healthy."

"I know you better than anyone, Mark. I know that you won't let yourself fall for someone new while we're still married. Not really. And you deserve someone who makes you happy and treats you right. If that's - um, Grayson? - then you should be with him. And I'm not going to be the thing holding you back."

He grabbed a pen off of a nearby table and signed the papers before handing them to me. "Thank you," I said, as I signed them myself. He was right, of course. It would take another three months once we actually filed the papers before a judge could officially grant us a divorce. But knowing that we'd both agreed to it and accepted it made me feel a lot better about starting something with Grayson in the meantime.

"So," he said sadly. "My mom is dying."

"I'm sorry," I said, putting a hand on his shoulder. "I'm glad you're here while she still has time."

"Me too. I just feel like an ass. Why didn't I come around more?"

"Because your father was an abusive monster and they were all terrible to you when we got married," I reminded him. "Don't be so hard on yourself, Adam. Just make the most of the time you have left. I would give anything to have known that my dad was going to die ahead of time so that I could have spent more time with him before it happened."

He squeezed my hand then led me into the kitchen where Hattie and Scotty were preparing lunch. We helped them finish up and for the first time, I felt like part of the family. Too bad it was too late.

We took Adam to another AA meeting that afternoon in a neighboring city, hoping to avoid any more run-ins with people he knew. It went fairly well. Though he was still too afraid to speak himself, he seemed reinvigorated in his desire to get clean.

That night I texted Grayson to tell him that Adam and I had signed the divorce papers. I wanted to call and hear his voice, but I also didn't want to hurt Adam's feelings if he overheard us. Grayson told me he was happy that Adam and I had worked out our differences, and sent me an adorable picture of him and Dolly at the park. I sat for a while looking at it and Scotty, who moves more quietly than any person I've ever met, saw it over my shoulder as he entered the room behind me.

"Moving on already?" he asked as he sat at the kitchen table next to me.

"In some ways, I guess. In others, not so much."

"Thank you for comin'. I gathered from what Adam told me and Momma that he doesn't particularly deserve your help," he said.

"Well, somebody told me recently that none of us deserve anything," I recalled Grayson's words. "But if we're lucky, people love us anyway. I'll always love Adam, even if we aren't *in* love."

"I hope I find that someday," he said wistfully.

"I'm sure you will. It's a lot easier when you're honest with yourself like you have been recently. And it helps that a lot more people are comfortable being out now."

"It must have been a lot worse coming out when you were my age," he said.

"I'm not *that* old Scotty," I laughed. "But yeah, I guess, it was hard to come out to some people. I was lucky that my father was very supportive."

"He wasn't upset at all?" he asked, wide-eyed.

"I'm sure he was at first," I admitted. "It took him a few minutes to say anything. He just stared at the floor for a while. But after the shock wore off, he looked at me and he said, *Mijo*, this life is not about who we love. It's about *how* we love. And I love you no matter what.' And that was it. He went right back to being my dad like nothing had changed."

"Sounds like my momma," he said sadly.

"I've always known your mother was a good one, Scotty," I said, squeezing his arm. "I'm so sorry for what's happening to her."

His eyes watered a bit as he said, "I don't know what I'm gonna do without her."

"I'll tell you what you're going to do. You're going to move in with Adam, finish school, become a doctor, and make your mother proud. If your other brothers come around, great. If not, screw 'em. You don't need them to live a good life."

He smiled at me and wiped his eyes. Hattie entered the room and Scotty excused himself to go to bed.

"I sure was sorry to hear about your daddy, Mark," she said. "Always seemed like a real nice man."

"Thank you, Hattie. He was," I said. "How are you feeling? I'm sorry you're going through this."

"Oh, I've been through worse, baby," she said, easing herself slowly down onto a chair. "Hell, I'm going through worse worrying about whether my boys will ever be a family or not once I'm gone."

"I know, I'm sorry. I wish I could say I believe they will be. But I'm not sure this is a difference they can overcome."

"It's a big one, isn't it?" she asked. I nodded and she continued. "Baby I'm real sorry we weren't more supportive of you and Adam. I always thought you were nice. But I tell you what, the church drills ideas into you and it's hard to let 'em go. Now that Scotty came out too, I've been wonderin' a lot about God lately. You know they say He don't make mistakes. So if He made two of my baby boys gay, I can't believe that there's anything wrong with it. I wish to God every day Ricky had died sooner. Maybe I would have had more time to fix things with Adam."

"I'm here now," Adam's voice said from the dark hallway. He entered the room and wrapped his arms around Hattie. "I'm sorry it took me so long, Momma. But I'm here now. And I'm gonna be with you until the end."

The next 30 days were a test of fortitude for all four of us in different ways. Adam's family and I accompanied him to as many AA meetings as we could find, and helped keep him accountable and away from any alcohol. I had a few setbacks with my OCD that almost sent me packing, but Grayson was able to calm me down over the phone. Hattie had it the worst, of course. She had a few health rebounds, but inevitably got sicker each time after a few days. Scotty, meanwhile, was studying for finals and working out his transfer to the university where Adam taught amidst all of this.

On the lighter side of things, we all decorated the house for Christmas together, and on one of Hattie's good days I managed to get a great picture of her with Scotty and Adam in front of the tree. I had it blown up for her and hung it beside her bed.

A few days before Christmas, Adam was presented with a coin to celebrate 30 days of sobriety from his sponsor, an older woman named Louise. For the first time, he spoke in front of the group that day.

"Thank you all so much," he began after introducing himself. "I guess this is as good a time as any to finally tell my story. It started when my marriage ended. It was my choice, but I wasn't prepared for how lonely it would be. I made some mistakes in the early days of the separation that made me feel lonelier, and alcohol numbed that pain. So I drank, and I drank some more. And eventually I drank so much that I pushed away anyone who tried to help me.

"But I couldn't see that that's what was happening. I kept telling everyone I was fine. But I wasn't. And the crazy thing was that I truly thought that I was. I wholeheartedly believed that I was just a casual drinker and that everyone around me was overreacting. In my head everything I was doing was totally fine, and I wanted so badly for that to be true that I didn't notice I was becoming the villain in my own story. I mistreated people who love me and people who might have. I took for granted the career I worked my whole life for. And I lost the love of my life."

He paused, looking at me with tears in his eyes, on the last sentence. I was trying to hold back tears myself, so I averted my gaze and he continued.

"But he's happy now. At least, I think he is. I *hope* he is, because he made me so happy all of the years we were together. So I'm going to try to be happy too. And I'm home with my family, repairing relationships that I never thought I would get the chance to repair. And I haven't had a drink in 30 days. So I feel like I'm on a good path now. No matter what happens from here, I have hope. And after not having any for a long time, hope feels like an awful lot to have. You all gave me that. Thank you."

The group applauded, and Adam returned to his seat with a new spring in his step. A weight lifted from his shoulders. When we arrived back at his mother's house, I pulled him aside before we went in.

"You'll never lose me, Adam. Not completely," I said. "Maybe things will work out with Grayson, and maybe they won't. But not matter what, you and I can be friends, if you want to be."

"I would love that," he said. He hugged me and went inside just as my phone began to ring. It was Grayson. He and I had kept in touch as best we could over the month I'd been gone, but it had been a few days since we spoke on the phone instead of through text message, so I was excited to hear from him.

"Hi there," I greeted him happily.

"Hey," he said solemnly. I had very rarely heard Grayson sound anything other than happy.

You aren't even officially dating and he's calling to break up with you. You must be more terrible than you thought. I made myself recall Grayson telling me I was strong again and pushed forward with the conversation.

"Oh, what's wrong?" I asked.

"Nothing, I'm fine."

"Grayson, you can tell me," I insisted.

"Well, my parents are leaving town for Christmas I guess," he said with a deep sigh. "They're going to visit my dad's parents in Seattle. They didn't tell me until today and they offered for me to go with them, but I already put up signs all over town saying I'd be opening the diner to the homeless again. I can't go back on that. At least I won't be alone, but I haven't missed Christmas with my parents since Alex died."

"I'm sorry, Grayson. Is there anyone who could watch the diner for you for a few days?"

"I haven't asked," he admitted. "I hate to ask

anyone to give up their Christmas for me. Oh crap,
I gotta go. I let Trey fill in for you while you've been
gone and he filled up the place with smoke – again.
Anyway, I just wanted to hear your voice. Talk to you
soon?"

"Yeah, sure. Call me when you can."

I hung up and went inside. Adam knew
something was wrong just by looking at me, so I
explained the situation. He disappeared back into the
room where Hattie kept her old computer and returned
having bought me a plane ticket.

"Go," he said. "Be with him, or cover for him so
he can go with his parents – whatever you want to do.
But you've done enough for me. It was so incredible of
you to come here and be with me and my family
through this. But it's over. I'm good. I promise. Now it's
your turn. I'll even drive you."

I arrived back home shortly after the diner had
closed, and used the emergency key Grayson had given
me to sneak in. I had only intended to bake him a cake
as a surprise, but I found the diner completely
undecorated for the season. I hurried to a store, bought

decorations, and returned, careful not to cross too close to the cottage where he could see me. I set a cake from his favorite recipe to bake and then went about decorating the whole diner as I waited for it.

After everything was ready, I set up candles around one of the tables and called Grayson.

"Hey, you," he said, trying to sound happy, but failing.

"Hey, handsome," I said.

"Oh, no," he said, sounding a bit better. "I look terrible today."

"I'm absolutely positive that you don't," I assured him. "Listen, I had somebody deliver a Christmas gift for you, but they left it at the front door of the diner. I don't want somebody else to take it. Would you mind running up to get it?"

"Aw, seriously? That's so sweet. Okay, I'm going right now. What are you up to?"

"Oh, not a whole lot. I just finished making a cake and setting up some Christmas decorations," I said, choosing my words carefully so as not to lie to him.

"I wish you were here to decorate the diner," he said. I could hear him shutting the door to the cottage and went and stood by the front door of the diner to wait for him. "I just haven't been feeling it this year."

"I'm sorry. Maybe your gift will cheer you up just a bit."

"Well, it's from you, so I'm sure it will be-" he trailed off as he rounded the corner and saw me standing at the door. He ran excitedly into the diner and wrapped his arms around me. I picked him up and spun him around, not an easy feat given his height.

"Amazing," he finished his thought.

"I knew you didn't look terrible," I said, stepping back to look at him. He looked just as good as I remembered him, still perfectly groomed and well dressed. However, he was wearing his glasses and his eyes behind them looked puffy as if he'd been crying.

"What are you doing here?" he asked.

I had intended to say that I'd come home to spend the holiday with him. But I knew looking at him that he needed his family, and he had been so selfless with me that I felt like it was my turn to be so for him.

"I came to cover the diner so you can spend Christmas with your parents," I said.

"What? Are you serious?"

"I absolutely am. But first, I have something for you. Come with me." I led him to the table where I'd put out his cake and set a Christmas playlist to play on my phone. A few days prior, I'd gone to the mall back in Texas with Scotty to go Christmas shopping. I'd agonized over what to get Grayson, and finally settled on a pocket watch. Inside behind the hands, I'd had a picture of him and his brother, Alex, put in. "This is your real gift," I said, presenting him with the box.

As he opened it, he smiled at the watch. But when he actually opened the watch and saw the picture inside, his eyes welled up instantly. "It's so beautiful," he said, standing to hug me. "Thank you, Mark. I love it."

"You're welcome," I whispered, holding him tight.

"I didn't get you anything yet," he said with a frown. "I'm sorry. I've just been feeling down and I didn't know when you were coming back."

"Hey, you've given me all I could ever need," I said, cupping his face in my hands. "Except maybe one thing. I pointed above us to show him that we were standing directly under mistletoe.

He smiled through his tears and kissed me. And this time, with nothing to hold us back, I kissed him back even more passionately. I felt like I was high on kissing him, like the room was spinning around me and my heart was beating so fast it might burst out of my chest like a cartoon. I rested my head on his chest and we swayed to the music. I was so lost in him that I almost didn't notice when the candles set off the sprinkler system.

He stepped away, smiled at me, and said exactly what I'd been thinking the first time we kissed, "This must be what magic feels like."

Chapter Nine | *Adam*

It hadn't been easy to let Mark go, especially after having spent a month with him helping me stay sober. With my mind clear I could see that I still loved him. But he was falling for someone else, someone who loved him better than I could. The funny thing about love is that it makes you want to do what's best for the ones you feel it for, even if it means letting them go.

So I focused on my family. Scotty and I called over and over to beg Drew and Mitch to come to the house for Christmas, but they wouldn't budge. Drew, always the more stubborn of the two, was angrier each time we tried. I thought for a minute that Mitch, the gentler, more forgiving twin, might give in. But Drew must have gotten to him because he just stopped answering after a few tries.

So Scotty and I did everything we could to

make the week leading up to Christmas special for our mother. We decorated every inch of the house. We invited the children's choir from her church to the house to sing carols for her. We made all of her favorite foods and watched the Christmas cartoons she'd watched with us when we were children. She did her best to pretend it was perfect, but I knew she missed my brothers.

The morning of Christmas Eve, as it became clear that she didn't have much time left, I flew into Austin. Mitch lived there, Drew in San Antonio. I was determined to bring them back with me.

I started with Drew. I knew that he'd be harder to convince, but that if I showed up at Mitch's house with him in tow, Mitch wouldn't hesitate to join us. When I arrived at Drew's house, he was outside scraping ice off of his car windows.

It had been so long since I'd seen him that I almost forgot what he looked like. He favored my father much more than my mother, unlike Scotty and me. As I pulled into the driveway, I saw disgust wash over his face when he recognized me from his seat on the porch swing. By the time I stepped out of the car I'd rented to get to him, he was at the door ready to confront me.

"What the hell do you want?" he demanded.

"Good to see you too, brother," I snapped.

"Cut the bullshit, Adam. Why are you here?"

"You cut the bullshit, Drew," I shouted, the mean streak in me surfacing quicker than I'd expected. But I didn't have time to play games. "You know why I'm here. Momma is dying, and she wants to see you and Mitch before she goes. I don't give a fuck if you like me, but you owe it to her to say goodbye. So either get in the car on your own, or I can throw you in the back after I kick your ass. You choose. But one way or another, you're going."

"Drew," called a voice from just inside the front door before he could reply. Sarah, Drew's wife of seven years, stepped outside. She was pregnant, pretty far along by the look of it, with what would be their first child. She waddled over toward us, her blonde hair shimmering as sunrise began. "Go," she told him.

"Sarah," he began to protest.

"Andrew Theodore King, you get your butt in

that car with your brother right now. When this baby comes, I want her to have a family. You don't get to ruin that because you're stubborn," she said. "Hey Adam." She awkwardly stepped closer and gave me a quick hug. Sarah and I had always gotten along, even when Drew and I hadn't.

"Hey, nice mom voice. You're ready to go," I joked.

"Thanks Uncle Adam," she said rubbing her belly. "I wish I could go with y'all but I'm in the no travel zone. This little girl is about ready to drop outta me. Oh, she's kicking. You can feel if you want."

"Wow," I said as I felt her stomach, trying to ignore Drew rolling his eyes at me. "How much longer?"

"Two more weeks," she said smiling. "I can't wait."

"Congratulations, I'm so happy for you both," I said.

"Thank you, Adam. You," she snapped her fingers at Drew. "Go pack a bag. You're going."

Drew begrudgingly marched inside and Sarah and I caught up while we waited for him. He returned a few minutes later with a small bag, hanging up his phone. "Mitch is waiting," he grunted.

"Be nice," Sarah said before she kissed him goodbye.

I said goodbye to her and got back into the driver's seat while Drew crammed his long legs into the small back seat to avoid having to sit by me. We drove the almost two hours to Austin in complete silence. We picked up Mitch, who as I expected didn't put up a fight since Drew was with me, and drove to the airport in the same silence. Both of them sat in the backseat this time.

I paid for their tickets and made sure to get them seats far away from mine. When we finally made it back home, Scotty and Momma met us outside.

"What are you doing? You need to be in bed," I told her.

"No offense baby, but shut the hell up," she said. "All four of my boys are here, and I'm not wastin' this time. Get your butts back in the car. We're going to dinner."

"Momma, you can barely stand," I said.

"Do I look like I care, boy?" she snapped, gasping for air between words. "We're going. You're not too old for me whip your little behind. Now are you gonna drive or does Scotty need to?"

I looked at Scotty and he mouthed, "I tried," and shrugged. So all five of us piled back into the car, just like when we were kids. We drove to my mother's favorite restaurant and found it empty. The owner, a member of my mother's church, had shut the place down so that my mother could have one last dinner out with her family in peace.

We ate almost silently. Our mother seemed to just enjoy being in the presence of all four of us. But it was difficult for any of us to enjoy ourselves knowing that she was getting so much worse. It didn't help that two of the four other people at the table hated me either.

After dinner we drove our mother around town to see the Christmas lights in the fancier neighborhoods. She cried as she watched the lights at one of the bigger houses, and that was the moment I knew that she could feel her time running out.

I drove us all home and helped her get settled. She insisted on staying out in the living room to be near everyone instead of going to her room. So I tucked her in to blankets on the couch and we all gathered around her and talked with her until she fell asleep. Mitch and Drew continued their game of pretending Scotty and I weren't there until Scotty finally couldn't handle it anymore.

"Are y'all still mad at me?" he asked. "I'm really sorry. I wish I wasn't gay but I just am."

"No, Scotty, don't apologize to them for being who you are," I said. "And you two should be ashamed of yourselves for shutting him out. It was bad enough you did it to me but he's your little brother. You're supposed to look out for him."

"You mean like you did for us?" Mitch asked, rolling his eyes.

"What is that supposed to mean?" I snapped.

"You really think we're mad at Scotty for being gay?" Drew butted in. "We were mad at him for being like *you*."

"But that wasn't cool," Mitch added. "We're sorry, Scotty. We know you aren't really a garbage person like Adam. We don't care if you like dudes."

"Yeah, little man. We're sorry. We shouldn't have shut you out. *Adam* is the one we really have a problem with. He abandoned us," Drew said.

"Whoa, whoa, hold on," I finally managed to get in. "What do you mean I abandoned you?"

"Adam, what else did you do when you came out?" Drew asked.

"I can answer that," Mitch said.

"Will one of you please just explain," I said, tiring of their back and forth routine. They started playing rock, paper, scissors. "Oh my god, you're children. Drew, speak."

"You left, Adam," he said. "You were already 18, so when Dad didn't like what you had to say about yourself, you just took off. But me and Mitch were only 13. We were still kids. But you being gone made us the oldest. So who do you think started taking beatings when Dad got drunk?"

"You were big enough to defend yourself when he went after you," Mitch took over. "We weren't. He beat us black and blue until we were finally grown enough to fight back. And when we were old enough to move out, we stayed close in case Momma and Scotty needed us. We didn't leave town until that son of a bitch was dead. But you were long gone."

"We thought you'd come back for us," Drew picked back up. "We thought our big brother would come save us. But you never did. We don't hate you because you're gay, Adam."

"We hate you because you're selfish," Mitch finished the thought. "And when you married Mark it was like you were leavin' us even further behind than you already had. Momma and Dad might have had wanted you to be straight. But all we ever wanted was for you to care about us."

That one hurt, but I knew they were right. I had been so focused on my own survival that I hadn't considered that I was leaving them to fend for themselves. I ran away because it was what I needed, but I forgot about what they needed. And I'd done the same thing to Mark. Perspective is a real pain in the ass sometimes.

"I'm so sorry," I said. "Truly, I am. You're right. I was selfish. I was so afraid of dealing with Dad that I just took off and didn't think about what he might do to you. And that was wrong. I should have stayed and made sure you were okay. And I should have made more of an effort to be close to you all after Mark and I got together."

"We know," they said in unison.

"Give him a break," Scotty suddenly spoke up. All three of us turned to focus on him. "He was scared. And he was still a kid. He made a crappy choice, and he made some crappy choices after that. But he's here now, and he's still our brother."

"He's right, babies," Momma said, stirring. "You all need each other. I want y'all to know how sorry I am for not getting us away from your daddy. I made my choices out of fear just like Adam did. And Adam, I'm so sorry that I didn't support you coming out. Maybe if I had spoken up for you, you'd have stuck around. But I know all four of you remember how your daddy was. Y'all can't go holding the way he made you act against each other. He messed all of us up in different ways. And when I'm gone, you four are gonna need each other if you ever wanna be whole again. And babies, I think that time might be comin' sooner than we'd like."

"Remember how we used to play *Monopoly* when Dad worked late?" Mitch asked, trying to avoid the inevitable.

"I still keep it in the same place," Momma said, smiling as she sat up straighter.

"I'll get it," Drew said, getting up to go. "Scotty can't play. I'm still upset that he ate the car piece."

"I was literally 2 years old," Scotty yelled, following him out.

Mitch stayed put, but extended his hand to me, "We're good," he said. "Well, maybe not yet. But someday."

"Thank you," I said, shaking his hand. "I'll earn your forgiveness. I promise."

"If you have any leads on a job or a free apartment, that'd be a good start," he said. "Oil industry is not what it used to be and I have about two weeks to find steady work or somewhere to crash before my ass is on the street. What are you smiling at?"

"I might have an idea," I explained, as Drew and Scotty reentered the room arguing over who was going to get to use the hat game piece.

"You crapped out the car, little man. Nobody wants to use that now. I don't know why it's even in the box still," Drew was saying.

"It's been 20 years," Scotty shouted. "Even if it hadn't been cleaned, I'm pretty sure fecal matter doesn't have any effects that last that long."

"Well, when you're a hotshot doctor you can let us know. Until then, you get the dumbass thimble," Drew replied.

"Hey, Scotty," I said. "What do you think about another roommate?" I gestured at Mitch, who swapped the confused look on his face for one of surprise.

"I dunno. These two basically share 80 percent of their personality and Drew is being a real dick right now," Scotty said.

"Wait, you guys are moving in together?" Drew

asked.

I nodded and Mitch said, "I'm in. If it's okay with Scotty."

Scotty rubbed his chin thoughtfully before saying, "I'm gonna say hard pass, but thanks for the offer."

Mitch jumped up off the floor and wrapped Scotty in a headlock. Drew sat down next to Momma and rested his head on her shoulder as he watched our brothers wrestle like children. I watched them all and finally felt like my family was at peace again. Maybe not even again. Maybe for the first time. Despite the issues we'd had with each other, we were losing our mother. We knew that, and in the face of it, all that mattered was that we were family.

"Ow, ow, okay he can come," Scotty conceded when Mitch got him pinned down.

"So it's settled, then," I said. "You two dummies are coming home with me. Now, are you all ready to lose this game?"

"I hope you're ready too, baby," Momma said. "I want you all to know before I whip your butts that I love you all very much. I'll always be with you."

So we played. All night. We joked and laughed, cheated and argued, ate junk food and slowly healed some of the many wounds my father had left for us. My mother was the happiest I'd ever seen her. Her smile bright and full despite how sick she was. Her laugh louder than ever.

So, when we awoke late on the afternoon of the 28th and discovered that she had passed quietly in her sleep, I chose to remember her the way she had been that night. Beautiful, happy, and free, strong in the face of the ultimate adversity.

I hadn't expected the funeral to be much more than my three brothers and me because it fell on New Year's Eve, but I far underestimated the presence Hattie King had in that town. Her small church was overflowing with people who wanted to pay their respects. Even Mark flew down to stand by my side as I said goodbye. I didn't know it until after he'd already gone home, but he'd also secretly paid for the funeral. When I asked him why, he simply replied, "She was a good woman. She was family."

We buried our mother late in the morning, then returned back to her favorite restaurant to have another family dinner in her honor. Though this one was a much heavier occasion, there was far less tension in the room, as the four of us shared our favorite memories of our mother.

Midway through dinner, however, Drew got a call – Sarah was going into labor early. We put Drew on a plane and the rest of us drove down together to meet our new niece. And so, in the early hours of the morning after our mother was laid to rest, her first grandchild was born. A girl, named Abigail Hattie King.

Sarah, ecstatic to see that we were all getting along, invited Mitch, Scotty, and I to stay for a few days. So we did, doing as much as we could to help Drew finish up the preparations at the house since the baby had come early.

But we couldn't stay as long as we probably would have liked. Newly sober, I had a job to get back to. Scotty's transfer had also been approved; so he had classes to prepare for.

"Congratulations," I told Drew as we said goodbye. "Call me if you need anything. Anything at all."

"Thanks, I will," he said. I started to get into the car and he stopped me. "Hey, Adam? I love you, bubba. Don't be a stranger anymore, okay?"

"I love you too, little brother. And are you kidding me? I'm gonna be coming to see that baby at least six times a year," I said. "If you happen to be here too, maybe we can catch a movie or something."

I dropped Mitch off back in Austin to get his affairs in order and Scotty and I drove back home. It felt wrong to just abandon our mother's home, so we asked one of her close friends to keep an eye on it for us until we figured out what to do next. We spent a few days sorting through her things and making sure everything was settled. We mailed Drew a few of her things that we thought he'd want, took a few things for ourselves and Mitch, and then put the rest away safely.

"Crazy, isn't it?" Scotty asked as we loaded up boxes. "One day you're a person with this whole life. Then all that's left of you is packed away."

"This isn't all that's left of her, buddy," I said, setting down the box I was carrying so that I could hug him. "She raised four kids. Whatever we become isn't just for us. It's her legacy now too."

"You're pretty good at this big brother thing," he said, squeezing me tight.

"Yeah, well I've got a lot of lost time to make up for," I admitted.

When we got back to California, Scotty helped me get my apartment clean and cleared of all the liquor and we fixed the hole I'd made in the wall. We rearranged the best we could to make my one bedroom function for three grown men, though we weren't entirely sure how long it would be before Mitch joined us.

The following week, school began. Scotty threw himself into his course work with such focus that it helped inspire me to work even harder than I already knew I had to. I had, unsurprisingly, been knocked back down to only the three courses I normally taught. The newer courses I had tried to take on during the previous semester had been reassigned.

"I'm very pleased to have you back," Dr. Lewis had said when I presented her with my 30 day chip and asked for permission to return. "I did not relish in stripping you of your duties, Dr. King. But I trust you understand now that it was for your own benefit."

"I do, Dr. Lewis," I agreed. "It was the right call. I let you down. It won't happen again."

"Excellent. Well, let us get to work then," she said with a cordial smile.

My first two classes were seamless. I was so determined to do better that I was putting in more effort than I'd ever put into anything. The students appeared at least moderately interested, which was honestly the best I could hope for some semesters.

I was momentarily thrown, however, in my third class on the first day. Lauren, the pregnant student from the previous semester, was there. She must have been almost seven months pregnant by then. She had a hard time fitting her round belly in the cramped desk seat, so I set up a chair at a table up front for her. She eyed me suspiciously as she got situated, and continued to do so throughout my lecture. She wasn't the only one.

Throughout the day students had been whispering to each other as they stared at me.

"So, I know you've all probably heard a lot about me," I said, facing the group of 30 students. "So I just want to clear the air so we can get through this semester without your inevitable questions being a distraction for you.

"So, first of all, yes it is true that I am alcoholic. It's also true that I was suspended last semester for some very poor decisions that I made both under the influence of alcohol and out of sheer stupidity. I've made a lot of mistakes in the last few months. But I'm still standing. It wasn't easy, but I worked out my issues and I am back and ready to try and do better.

"Now, I can't promise you that I'm going to be perfect. If you've heard even one of the rumors about me, and I'm sure have, you know that I'm far from it. But I can promise you that I want to be a good teacher. I want you to learn something from my class. And I can promise you that though I'll push you to do your best, I won't be hard on you when you make a mistake — because God knows I've made some big mistakes of my own.

"So, if you feel like you can trust me to guide you through this course, then I'd love to have you. But if you don't, I absolutely understand. And you're welcome to go now so that I don't waste your time." I gestured toward the door and waited.

A few students shifted in their seats, but no one actually left. So we continued with class. In honor of my mother, I asked the students to write about their parents. I was touched by most of their submissions, though they made me regret not making up with my own mother sooner.

Lauren's however, was far darker than the others. Like me, she'd had an abusive father. But he'd been far worse than mine. When she was 9, he'd beaten her mother to death. The realization of how much worse we could have had it made me appreciate having reconnected with my brothers even more.

I was beyond relieved when I finally finished the day's work and got to go home. I fixed dinner for Scotty and myself before he went with me to an AA meeting. Then we returned home where he worked on his homework and I prepared for the next day's classes.

We continued this pattern for the next month. There were several days where I badly craved a drink. I'd gotten so used to leaning on alcohol to deal with stress that it was like a default response to crave a drink when my day threw me anything unexpected. But Scotty kept me in line, dragging me to meetings as often as he needed to and coaching me through the cravings.

Mitch moved in at the beginning of February, and I helped him get enrolled in classes at the community college across town to work on getting a business degree. And so we worked him into our routine. Not that it was a huge change. One more person at dinner and then one more person sprawled out on the floor working afterward. We also worked out a weekly video chat with Drew and made plans to visit him at Easter.

Everything finally felt peaceful in my life, aside from Lauren still watching me in class like she was in CIA training. Things were good between Mark and me.

We didn't talk much, but when we did it was friendly. For the first time in my adult life I was not only on speaking terms with all of my brothers, but actually getting along with them really well. If that had been the way my life remained, I would have been perfectly happy. But as it so often does, life had another trick up its sleeve.

February passed rather uneventfully. Mitch and Scotty both managed to find dates for Valentine's Day, but I just acted like it was any other day. Mark, having returned to his old law firm, set Mitch up with an assistant job for a few weeks, but that was the only real change for a while.

In the third week of March, however, several things happened all at once. First, I received a package from Mark. It contained our approved divorce decree from the judge and a letter. It read:

Adam,

This is it. It's official. I'm a little sad, but I think it's for the best. I hope you know I'll always love you. And to that effect, I want to give you something. Think of it as a farewell gift and a thank you. In this envelope

I've included the deed to the house. I want you and your brothers to have it. I'm so happy that you've reconnected with them. And I'm proud of you for staying sober and working through all of your problems.

Who knows, maybe you'll start a family in that house someday like you always wanted, if that's still what you want. I hope you get whatever it is that you do want. I'm truly sorry that I wasn't able to give it to you. But I want you to know, I wouldn't take back a single second of it because for every painful memory I might have of you, I have at least three beautiful ones. I'd do it all again in a heartbeat.

By the time you get this, the house will be empty. Feel free to move in whenever you'd like. Maybe invite us over for dinner sometime? I'll be sure to let you know what I think about the new decorating.

Love always,

Mark

I choked back tears as I read the letter. I couldn't believe that it was really, truly over. 20 years, punctuated by a single envelope. But I couldn't imagine a better resolution if it had to end. And of course it did. I'd set us down this path without thinking it through, and it had backfired. But Mark was happy, and I was on my way there – faster than I could have imagined.

My brothers and I spent most of that week packing and moving. Mitch offered to repair the hole in the foyer wall for me, since Mark had taken the painting that once covered it. I told him to leave it, that I'd find something else to cover it. "Some scars are worth having," I explained.

By Friday, I was so exhausted that there was no possible way I could have been prepared for what happened in my last class of the day. During the first half of the lecture, I kept noticing Lauren squirming uncomfortably. *She's pregnant,* I thought. *Just leave her alone.* So I continued and tried to ignore it until, about a half hour into class, she quickly walked out of the room, a panicked look on her face.

"Class dismissed," I said. "Keep working on your midterm papers, and I'll see you on Monday." I followed her out and down the hallway. "Lauren, hey, what's going on?"

"Oh, Dr. King. It's nothing, yeah, nothing, everything's fine," she said, still squirming.

I looked down and noticed a large stain on the front of her jeans. "Lauren, did your water break?" I asked.

"This? No, I um, small bladder, baby pressing against it, normal pregnancy stuff," she tried to lie. But the scream she let out as a contraction kicked in gave her away.

"Okay, we gotta get you to a hospital," I said.

"No, I can't. I can't have this baby yet," she said loudly, her voice echoing in the empty hallway.

"Yes, you can, Lauren. You have to," I said, putting a hand on her back and trying to guide her forward.

"No I can't. I don't have anyone to give it to," she shouted, jerking away.

I froze, confused as to how she could possibly not have chosen birth parents at this late stage. "What happened to the adoption agency?" I asked.

"I went," she said. "It's just, all of the parents are like Stepford families. And they all have like 8 kids already and it's like okay Jon and Kate, leave some for everybody else. And I just wanted to find someone nice and someone who makes mistakes like I do who will let this kid be a kid and not a perfect little robot who gets perfect grades but never plays."

"Okay, Lauren, I'm sorry but you're out of time," I said as she hunched over from another contraction. "Social services can figure out the adoption for you, but right now you have to go deliver this baby."

"I can't. I can't," she kept whispering.

"Listen to me, Lauren," I said, taking her by the shoulders. "You can do this. You are so strong. I've read your papers. I know what you've been through. And this is gonna be over a lot faster than some of that stuff was. So we're gonna go to the hospital, and you're gonna deliver this baby. And I'll stand right there with you and you just squeeze my hands as hard as you need to. But you are going to do this. You can, and you have to. Okay?"

She nodded nervously and I again started guiding her forward. I helped her ease into the backseat of my car and sped as carefully as I could to the hospital. Her labor progressed quickly. By the time we got to the hospital her contractions were less than three minutes apart. Within two hours, she delivered a healthy, beautiful baby boy.

"Would you like to hold your son?" one of the nurses asked her when it was over.

"He's not my son," she said. The nurse nodded and started to take the baby out. "He belongs to him," she said. I looked down to see her pointing at me.

"Lauren, what the hell are you talking about?" I asked, clutching the side of her hospital bed.

"He's yours, if you want him," she said. "I can do that, right? I haven't signed away my rights or anything. So I can do that, can't I?"

"I have no idea, Lauren, but I can't raise a baby. I can barely take care of myself," I said.

"Yes, you can," she said, wiping sweat from her brow. "I've been watching you. Everybody in your classes knows how bad you fucked up last semester. But you've worked so hard to get yourself back on track that everyone just listens to you anyway. You make mistakes, just like me. But you learn from them, and you teach other people from them. That's what I want for this baby. And I know you want a baby. The adoption agency lady couldn't shut up about you when I told her you referred me."

"Lauren, I-," I stammered.

"Excuse me folks, but what am I doing with this baby?" the nurse asked.

"Give the baby to him," Lauren said. "Dr. King, if you can hold that baby and honestly tell me you don't fall in love right away, I'll sign whatever social services wants me to. But if you can't, I want you to take him, and raise him as well as I know you can."

I hesitated, but ultimately nodded at the nurse. A fatal mistake. I lost the battle as soon as she handed him to me. With him in my hands, I felt like a piece I didn't even know was missing had clicked into place. It felt right. He felt like mine.

"Hi," I whispered through tears. "It looks like I'm gonna be your daddy."

"I knew it," Lauren said smugly. She lay back and closed her eyes. "Be good to him. Love him."

"I will," I said. "I always will."

I waited to call anyone until I had spoken with one of Mark's legal colleagues and confirmed that it was in fact legal for Lauren to declare that I could adopt the baby there in the delivery room. I also checked with her to make sure she was okay with it again.

With everything settled, and the perfect little bundle of joy officially mine, I called my brothers. They thought I was joking. I had to have someone take a picture of me with the baby and send it to them. Mitch and Scotty came right over. Drew caught the next flight out and was there within hours.

"I knew you were always jealous of me, brother, but I didn't think you were *this* jealous," Drew said when he walked in to see me sitting in a rocking chair holding the baby.

"Shh," I said, rocking gently back and forth as all of my brothers stood around me. "I don't want him to know we're a bunch of assholes yet. He shouldn't learn that for a few years at least."

"Okay, but really, how do you just go to work one day and end up with a kid?" he asked. I explained what had happened with Lauren and he responded, "Sounds like one of Sarah's Lifetime movies, dude. But if you're happy, I'm happy."

"Kid is handsome like his uncles," Mitch said, making silly faces at the baby.

"That's literally impossible," Scotty said.

"It's a figure of speech, little man," Mitch replied.

"It's not," Scotty retorted. "It's really not."

They continued to bicker and Drew probably joined in, but I couldn't say for sure because I looked down at that wonderful little miracle in my arms and everything else faded away. I had a son. I'd been waiting for him for so long. He came in a way that I never could have predicted, but there he was - my son. I felt like my DNA had been fundamentally altered - like more than I was anything else from that moment on, I was that baby's father.

A nurse came in and offered to take a picture. So my brothers crowded around me and the nurse took the first ever photograph of me with all of my brothers where all four of us looked happy. I never could have imagined that a picture like that would exist, much less that it would include my child too.

I stayed at the hospital all weekend, until the baby was cleared to go home. I had Scotty pick up a car seat for me, but I didn't have a single other thing for the baby, so I was nervous on the way home. I almost stopped to pick a few things up, but I didn't have any way to carry the baby around and shop, so I planned to pick up one of my brothers and go back.

But when I opened the door to the house, there were two surprises waiting for me. First, all of the remaining boxes had been unpacked. My brothers had finished getting the house settled and it looked like an actual home. Second, sitting on the entry way table was a diaper bag with a note attached.

Adam,

Took Drew out for pizza because he wouldn't shut up about being hungry. Check out your awesome nursery upstairs. We got everything you should need. Don't worry, Sarah picked most of it out. Mitch and Scotty promise to babysit whenever you need in exchange for living here with you for free.

We love you jackass. Congrats,
Drew, Mitch, and Scotty

Right above the table, covering the patch in the
wall in the space where that old painting had once
hung, was a framed enlargement of the picture from the
hospital. We all looked so happy. We looked like a real
family. I felt like everything was in its right place. My
world, so full of turmoil for so long, had finally settled
and a peace had washed over it.

I don't think I'd ever meant something as
sincerely as I did as I looked from the picture to my son
and whispered, "It's perfect."

Chapter Ten | *Mark*

When I returned from Hattie's funeral, Grayson was still in Seattle with his parents. I tried to stay busy at the diner, making sure everything was taken care of so he wouldn't have anything to worry about when he came back.

As midnight approached, I settled onto the sofa at home to watch the New Year's Eve specials on TV. Even though Adam had been gone a while, this was the first holiday I was spending completely alone, and it felt odd.

Alone, just like you deserve to be.

I decided to bake brownies to keep myself busy. I started gathering ingredients only to realize that I was out of flour. So I walked down to the diner to borrow some. But as I approached, I noticed a light on in the cottage. Grayson's car was in the drive way, but he had left it there while he was out of town. He hadn't said anything about coming home.

Someone's in there. They're going to kill you.

I counted my fingers and reminded myself that Grayson thought I was strong. I slowly approached the cottage and tried to peek inside. I couldn't see anyone. I moved to the front door and turned the knob as quietly as possible. It opened, so I crept inside. Suddenly, Dolly came barreling around the corner from the bedroom.

"What is it, girl?" Grayson called after her as he entered the room wearing only a towel around his waist. "Oh, hey. Damn, I was going to surprise you in a little bit."

"You're here," I said excitedly. I wanted to rush into his arms, but we'd been taking things slow. This was the first time I'd ever even seen him without a shirt on. The visual was nice - *very* nice, but I was unsure how to proceed.

Grayson mercifully didn't overthink things as much as I did. He rushed forward as well as he could in the towel. He grabbed me and kissed me so passionately my knees went weak. Luckily, he had a good grip. He picked me up and carried me back to his bed. As we fell onto the bed and continued kissing, I ran my fingers through his hair and felt something sticky. I pulled my hand away to discover it was cookie dough.

"You know, I've always wondered how you got your hair so shiny," I said. "But I would never have come up with this as the answer."

"That was supposed to be part of the surprise," he said. He tickled me and I jumped off of him, only for him to move on top of me. "I accidentally turned the mixer on high and it went *everywhere*. I thought I had gotten all of it out of my hair." He laughed as he kissed me again, then rested his head on my chest.

"What are you doing home already?" I asked, rubbing his back.

"I missed you," he admitted, looking up at me. "I waited so long for you to come home just to leave you myself. I couldn't wait to get back and tell you that I love you."

I smiled at him full of joy as I said, "I love you

too."

"Good, then the cookie dough on my ceiling is worth it," he said as he tried to tickle me again. I rolled over on top of him and pinned his arms above his head to stop him. A look of panic washed over his face.

"Are you okay?" I asked, quickly letting him up. He scrambled to sit against the headboard. He looked embarrassed.

"I'm sorry," he said, his voice quivering.

"Grayson, it's fine. I'm sorry. I didn't mean to scare you," I said, scooting away to give him space. "I'm really, really sorry."

"It's not you, Mark," he said, drawing his knees up to his chest. "I have to tell you something."

"You can tell me anything, Grayson," I said. "Can I sit next to you?" He nodded so I sat on the bed next to him and held his hand.

"After Alex died," he said, squeezing my hand. "I was in a really dark place. I started dating this guy, Jack. I knew he wasn't a great guy. I met him at a club and somebody warned me about him before we left together that night. But I didn't care much about anything at the time so I ignored them. Everything was fine for a while, but the longer we dated, the more serious he became about me. And he started to get..."

He paused, tears running down his face. He looked away from me to wipe his eyes. "He started to hit me. It was nothing major at first. We got into an argument and he punched me in the arm. He apologized over and over and I really believed he was sorry. But it kept happening, and it kept getting worse. I broke up with him a few times, but he always threatened to kill me if I didn't come back."

He started to cry harder so I wrapped my arms around him. "Then one night, he wanted to have sex. But he'd already hit me earlier that day, so I wasn't having it. So he started hitting me again. Harder than he ever had before. Then he pinned me down and... and he..." his voice broke and he couldn't continue. He buried his face in my neck and cried.

"Grayson, I'm sorry," I said, my own eyes filling with tears. "I had no idea. I'm so, so sorry. Is he... still out there?"

He shook his head. "When I finally got up the

nerve to tell my parents, they called the police. Turned out he had warrants for other things, so he's in prison."

"Good," I said. "I hope he rots there." I was angrier than I'd ever been in my life. The idea that someone could take advantage of Grayson that way made my blood boil. I held onto him tightly until he was calmed down.

"I'm sorry I didn't tell you sooner," he said after a while. "I was too ashamed."

"Ashamed? Grayson, you didn't do anything wrong," I reassured him.

"You don't think I'm weak for letting that happen to me?" he asked, sounding surprised.

"Are you kidding me? I meant it when I told you that I love you," I said, shifting to look him in the eyes. "You are so incredible in my eyes. Nothing could ever change that. And you aren't weak. You're the strongest man I know. And I would kill that bastard if he ever came near you again."

He laid his head down on my chest and sighed. "We can keep taking things slow," I said. "I just want to be with you. I'm okay waiting to be physical until you feel like you're ready."

"You'd really be okay with that?" he asked.

"Of course," I said. "I'd love you no matter what. Here, I think it's time I give this back to you." I pulled the handkerchief he had given me when we met out of my wallet and handed it to him. "So you'll know I'm always on your side."

He took the handkerchief, kissed me again, then fell asleep on my chest. Taking things slow was perfect for us. I really just wanted to spend time with him. Nothing else mattered to me.

A few weeks into January, I received a call from my old law firm. They had an open associate position and wanted to offer it to me on a probationary basis for six months. I turned it down initially, but Grayson wouldn't let me pass up the opportunity.

"You're fired," he told me when I walked into the diner the next day. "I'm serious. I'm not going to let you give up on your dream. You've worked your whole life for that career. You have to get it back. Besides, absence makes the heart grow fonder, right? That can only be a good thing for us."

"I don't know," I said. "I'm not sure my heart can handle any more fondness for you. It's pretty full as is."

He kissed me, then playfully slapped my butt and said, "Go be a lawyer again. And send me pictures of yourself in your suit - or out of it. Surprise me."

So I went. I handled mostly easy cases for a while to test the waters. After a couple of weeks, I was really getting into the swing of things and picked up a couple of high profile clients, which earned me the right to an assistant. Since Adam's brother Mitch had just moved to town and needed work, I tried him out. After everything, it felt like the right thing to do to try to mend fences with Adam's family as well. He learned quickly and helped me keep on top of things on the days when I struggled, so I was glad to have him.

Work in general was going well, much better than I'd expected, in fact. And not seeing Grayson all day like I was used to made the time I did get to spend with him, which was pretty much every evening, feel more special.

On Valentine's Day, we accidentally surprised

each other with tickets to the same movie. They were for different show times, so we saw it twice with dinner in between. Simple as it was, it felt special and romantic in our own little way. We made love for the first time that night and it was worth every minute that we'd waited.

"I love you," I whispered as I held him afterward.

"I love you too," he said, craning his head to kiss me.

"No, I mean I *really* love you," I said. "In a way I never thought I would love anyone again. My heart has been broken for so long that I almost couldn't remember what it felt like for it to be whole. But then you came along like the world's best heart surgeon and stitched me up so flawlessly that if I don't actively think about it, I don't even remember it ever being broken. You saved my life. And I don't think I can ever really repay you for that, but I'll spend as long as you let me trying."

He sat up and looked into my eyes. "Mark, I get it. I really do. Look, I may not have been as visibly broken when we met, but I was just coasting through my life. I spent every day missing my brother, and working just to keep myself from falling apart. And then you walked into the diner and you flipped a switch in me. All of a sudden, I actually *wanted* to get out of bed in the morning. I wanted to watch TV with you, and read books, and bake cookies, and even just sit in stillness and enjoy the quiet. I wanted every beautiful little second that you were willing to offer me. For the first time since Alex died, you gave me something to believe in. And if you'll have me, I'll keep believing in that for the rest of my life."

I kissed him again, knowing right then that I never wanted to let him go.

The rest of February passed by mostly uneventfully. But during the last week of the month, I was assigned to a pro bono case my firm had taken on to try to appear more philanthropic. The young man I would be representing, Bailey Hodges, was charged with attempted aggravated robbery for walking into a stranger's home and pulling a knife when they tried to confront him.

According to the arresting officers, he seemed to have no idea what was happening, and believed that the house was where he lived. He had been released on bail, but the assistant district attorney had been on a rampage and was not in a hurry to back down on any of his cases. So my firm took over the case for the overworked public defender that the court had assigned it to. I asked Mitch to set up a meeting with Bailey, but the address and phone number the police had provided us with turned out to be no good.

Mitch worked hard to track him down, but it still took over a week for us to discover that he was actually homeless. Mitch also found out that the house Bailey had broken into was one he had lived in as a child, and that he had been in and out of a mental health institution since he was 12 years old. When he'd turned 18 a couple of years before this incident, his parents had just taken off and left him behind.

It took a few days, but I tracked Bailey down at a homeless kitchen on the outskirts of town. He was in almost as bad condition as the facility itself. The building was in terrible disarray, with cracks in the walls and broken windows throughout, leaving the biting winter air to fill every room. The food they were being served looked worse than what he'd be eating if I couldn't spare him jail time.

Bailey was wearing a torn t-shirt with a thin jacket over it. He was covered in dirt and talking to himself. There was something familiar about him that I couldn't quite put my finger on. As I approached, I noticed something that broke my heart. He was counting his fingers.

He's crazy like you, you psychotic bastard.

He's not crazy. Neither am I. He just needs help, I thought to myself.

"Mr. Hodges? I'm Mark Diaz. I'm your attorney," I said, extending a hand to him. He looked me over and then closed his eyes and continued counting his fingers.

"1,2,3,4,5,6,7,8,9,10," he whispered. I had no idea what to do. It was like my brain was misfiring. I kept thinking of half ideas and then losing them. Finally, I remembered how Grayson had helped me on the day we met.

"So, my boyfriend has this really adorable dog," I said, sitting next to him. "When I first met them she was this tiny little poof ball. But now she's like a miniature horse, I swear. She's so big. Anyway, she does this really goofy thing when we get ready for bed at night where she has to prep her spot on the bed like she's out in the wild or something. She just walks around in a circle over and over until she decides it ready and then just throws herself down. The she howls, like legitimately howls, until we both give her a goodnight kiss on the top of her head. Do you want to see a picture of her?"

He nodded and I showed him a few pictures of Dolly with some kids who were playing with her at the diner. He smiled weakly. He clicked to the home screen of the phone and started playing the first game he found. I almost protested, but thought better of it. If it distracted him and helped him keep in control, I didn't have a problem with it.

"How about we go get you something a little more filling to eat?" I asked. He nodded emphatically and I helped him gather his things and take them to my car. We went to the Blue Moose Diner and I told him to order anything he wanted while I went to talk to Grayson.

"Oh my god. He looks like Alex," Grayson said when he saw Bailey. He took a step back and touched his hand to his chest.

"Oh, man. He does," I said as the realization clicked. Indeed, he bore a striking resemblance to Grayson's late brother. "I thought something was familiar about him earlier but I couldn't figure it out. I'm sorry Grayson. I can take him somewhere else."

"No, stay," he said, his face losing color. "He needs help. I'm just going to go lie down for a little bit."

"Hey, wait." I called after him as he started walking out. "I love you." I pulled him into a tight embrace. "I'll take him somewhere else as soon as he finishes eating. And then I'm going to come sit with you and take care of you. Okay? I love you, Grayson. I'm here for you."

"I love you too," he said, hanging his head. "I'm sorry. I just... wasn't prepared for that."

"I understand, sweetheart. I'm sorry," I replied, kissing his forehead "Get some rest. I'll be there soon."

He went back to the cottage and I returned to my table.

"I wasn't going to hurt anybody," Bailey said emphatically between bites of a cheeseburger as I settled into the booth across from him. "I swear. Sometimes I forget." He slapped his head three times in quick succession. "I used to live there, I think. I thought I still did and when that man came at me I got scared. That's all. Honest." He smacked his head again. I wanted to reach out and grab his hands to stop him, but I knew that would only make it worse.

"I believe you, Bailey. I promise, I do. Do you ever feel like you aren't entirely in control of what you're thinking or doing? Almost like your brain is a separate person making you do what it wants?"

He nodded enthusiastically. "All the time. I used to be smart, I think. I used to think about a lot of things. But now I only think about what my brain tells me to think. And it's usually scary stuff. Stuff I don't wanna see, but I can't stop it."

"Bailey, would you be willing to go to a doctor with me?"

"No, no, no. No doctors," he said quickly, smacking his head again. "They'll lock me away again."

"Hey, hey, Bailey, listen to me," I said, moving around the booth to sit next to him. "Look at me. I'm telling you right now, no matter what else happens, I'm not going to let anybody lock you up anywhere. I'm going to make sure you don't going to jail, and I'm going to get you the help you need to get back control of your brain. This doctor I want to take you to, she helped me. Okay? I used to have trouble making my brain listen to me too. I used to hear a voice telling me horrible things just like you do until she helped me."

"And now you don't hear the voice anymore?" he asked, his face full of hope.

"Well, I do sometimes," I admitted. "But I can usually make it go away a lot easier. She can help you learn to do that too. And she can give you medication that will help you manage it while you work on it."

"But I don't have any money," he said, his face

downcast.

"Don't worry about that. I'm going to help you, Bailey. I'm not going to let you go back out onto the street sick like this."

He smiled a crooked smile at me and finished his food, barely pausing for breath between bites. I drove him to Dr. Rodriguez's office and dropped him off. While he was speaking with her, I went back to check on Grayson. He was lying on the sofa crying, so I pulled him into my arms and held him until he stopped.

He asked me to drive him to the cemetery to visit his brother's grave, so I did. While he visited Alex, I walked over to my father's grave and sat down.

"Hi, Dad," I said. "I'm sorry it's been a while. It's been quite a year. I guess you know that though. At least, I like to think you're watching, from wherever you are. How self-centered is that, right? To think that you're in some amazing afterlife but you want to spend your time watching me? I just miss you, is all. I try to tell myself that you're always with me. It's sort of the only way I can keep breathing some days.

"Maybe it's silly, but I feel like I see you all around me. I see you every time I see a father and his child laughing out in town or even on TV. I hear you in all of your favorite songs when they come on the radio. I feel you with me when I'm in the kitchen. I see you in the stars at night, and I swear when the wind blows I can almost hear your voice. Wherever you are, I hope you know that I think about you every single day.

"So much has happened since you left, and all I want to do is pick up the phone and call you about every little thing, good and bad. And it kills me that I can't. I was thinking the other day about when I was a kid and your mom died. I think that might have been the only time I ever saw you cry. And it terrified me. I'd never seen you be anything but strong. But I know now that you *were* being strong. Because you got right back up and kept going. I know how hard that was for you now, because the grief I feel over losing you is boundless. I feel it in my bones. My soul aches when I let myself think for too long about the fact that you aren't here.

"And I wasn't as strong as you. Not by a long

shot. I gave up for a while there. It took someone special reminding me that you would want me to keep going to get me back on my feet. I like to think you had something to do with him ending up in my life. Like you're still looking out for me. Maybe that's silly too. But I know you'd love him, because he loves me. And he loves me so well. I think I'm going to marry him someday, Dad. I wish you could be here for that. But I know you'll be watching. And I know that you'll live on in the way that I love him back, because you taught me everything I know about how to love."

Grayson walked up, so I said goodbye to my father. I kissed my hand and touched it to the words, "Thomas Diaz, beloved father."

"You okay?" I asked, giving him a hug.

"Yeah," he said, smiling. "I feel a lot better. Thank you for bringing me."

"Of course," I said. "Anything you need. Forever."

"Forever?" he said, grinning.

"Yeah," I said. "If that's okay."

"Hm, I'll take it under consideration," he said,

wrapping one arm around my waist as we walked back to the car.

I dropped Grayson off at home, then picked up Bailey. I took him to pick up the medication that Dr. Diaz prescribed as well as a few changes of clothes and food. Then I dropped him off at a hotel and paid for a month up front.

Mitch helped me build my case over the next week, and at the beginning of March, we went before a judge. I argued that Bailey hadn't meant anyone any harm, and that he was not in a healthy state of mind at the time of the incident. I implored the judge to look at Bailey's history to see that he didn't need jail, just proper medical treatment. The ADA did his best to argue to the contrary, but in the end the judge agreed with me.

Even after only one week of treatment, Bailey was showing marked improvement. When I dropped him off at his hotel, he invited me in so that I could see some sketches he'd drawn. They were beautiful, vivid depictions of people and animals in the park across the street from the hotel.

"These are wonderful, Bailey," I told him.

"Take this one," he said, handing me a folded piece of paper. I unfolded it to find a drawing of me, Grayson, and Dolly.

"How'd you know this was my boyfriend?" I asked, stunned at how detailed it was.

"I saw the way you looked at him when you took me to lunch," he said matter-of-factly. "You love him. Big time."

"Yeah, big time," I said, smiling at the picture. "Thank you, Bailey."

Seeing the progress that Bailey was making gave me an idea. I went straight back to the office. "Mitch, do you trust me?" I asked as I entered in a hurry, digging through a filing cabinet for a contract.

"Well, I don't really know you that well yet," he said in his deep southern drawl. "But you seem pretty alright. I appreciate the job and everything."

"Great. You're fired."

"What the hell?" he exclaimed. "What did I do?"

I dropped his employment contract on his desk

in front of him and said louder, "It's just not going to work out, Mr. King. Pursuant to your employment agreement, we can pay you for six months of labor. You can stop by HR on your way out to organize payment." I leaned in to whisper to him, "Trust me. This will hold you over, and then I have more work for you. I'll call you in a few weeks." Confused, he wandered down the hall, looking back repeatedly as if he expected me to change my mind.

But I was setting a plan in motion. I was too afraid to tell anyone who didn't absolutely need to know about it until I had it all set, so I worked as secretly as possible to secure everything I needed.

In the meantime, I received mine and Adam's approved divorce decree in the mail. The county clerk's office had accidentally mailed both copies to my house. I sat at my desk staring at the envelope, unsure what to do next.

"Well, my marriage is officially over," I told Grayson as he entered the room.

He wrapped his arms around me from behind. "Are you okay? How do you feel?"

"You'd really be okay if I was upset about it, wouldn't you?" I asked, leaning back to kiss his cheek.

"Of course," he said. "Adam was a big part of your life. I'm sure he always will be."

"And you're okay with that?" I asked.

"I love every part of you, Mark. Even the messy parts," he said, kissing me on the forehead in the sweet way that he knew I loved.

"I love you so much, you know that? Do you want to move in together?" I asked.

"I thought you'd never ask," he said with a huge smile. He pulled a key out of his wallet. The word "home" was engraved on the top. "I've had this for weeks."

"You're so cute," I said, with a laugh. I swept him off of his feet and carried him upstairs to celebrate.

The next week, I moved into Grayson's cottage. I got all of the paperwork necessary to transfer the house over to Adam and mailed it to him with a letter and his copy of the divorce decree. Giving him that house felt like the right ending for that chapter of my life. I was ready to begin the next one with Grayson. If everything went how I was planning it, that chapter was already in the works.

I waited until the end of April when I was positive Mitch would be paid, and then I quit my job at the law firm. Throughout the preceding two months, I had secured the various parts of my plan so that I had it all ready to present to Grayson.

"Hey, babe. How was work?" he asked when I got home to the cottage that day. He was sitting at the kitchen table with a giant stack of receipts in front of him.

"It was fine," I said, planting a kiss on his cheek. "I quit."

"What?" he asked, dropping the pen he'd been holding.

"How busy are you right now?" I asked.

"Well I wasn't doing anything as important as discussing this."

"Come with me," I said, reaching my hand out to him.

He hesitated, but took my hand anyway and let me lead him. I drove him downtown and assured him as he attempted to discuss my job that he would understand when we got where we were going. We finally arrived at a fairly new but unmarked building.

"What is this, Mark?" he asked apprehensively as I opened his door for him.

"Come on, I'll show you," I said, taking his hand again and leading him inside.

I had already had most of the building furnished. There was a small reception area in the center of the lobby. Beyond that were several rooms. First was an office set up with the old office furniture from my house. Then a large room outfitted with computers and shelf after shelf filled with books, movies, and board games.

Then another office. This one contained a large desk, a sofa, and several comfy looking chairs. On the door, a sign read, "Dr. Hannah Rodriguez: Head Psychiatrist."

"Dr. Rodriguez got a new office?" he asked, confused. "Are you going to be her assistant or something?"

"Not exactly," I said. "Let's go upstairs." On the

five floors above were over 100 efficiency apartments.

"I don't understand," Grayson said as we headed back down to the main floor. "What exactly is going on here?"

"Remember Bailey, my client that reminded you of Alex?" I asked, leading him to sit in the lobby. "Well, Dr. Rodriguez has been working with him and he's gotten much better. And it got me to thinking about how many people don't have access to proper homes, much less mental health care. I was so lucky to have the resources that I did to be able to get the help that I needed.

"But there are so many people like Bailey and Alex who aren't as lucky. I want this to be a place where they can come for help. Dr. Rodriguez and a few other psychiatrists have agreed to volunteer their time for treatment. We'll give people homes until they're back on their feet. I'll run the administrative side of things. Bailey will be my assistant and Mitch will help set the tenants up with jobs. "

"I have so many questions," Grayson said, sitting down in the lobby area. "First, how did you manage to do all of this without me knowing? Second, how can you afford it?"

"I ran around like a maniac, basically," I admitted, taking his hands in mine. "And I secured a good amount of grant money. I have a few leads on other sources, and a few of my bigger clients from the law firm have agreed to partially fund us in exchange for being an honorary board of directors. I've thought it all out, babe. I promise. Are you okay? Are you upset? What are you feeling?"

"Are you kidding me?" he asked. "How could I be upset with you? Look what you did, Mark. This is so beyond incredible. I love it."

"Really?" I asked. He smiled and nodded, his eyes welling up. "Good, because there's one more thing I want to show you." I went behind the reception desk and retrieved a decal for the front door bearing the name of the home. "There's a big sign coming, but it takes an insanely long time to get those made, it turns out. But for now, I was hoping you'd do the honor of putting this on the door and making it official."

I handed him the decal and his eyes overflowed

with tears. "The Alexander Walker Refuge," he read, standing to hug me. "Mark, this is beautiful. I can't believe you did this."

I held him tightly and breathed a sigh of relief that he was happy. After he put the sign on the door, we stood outside to admire it. Well, he admired the sign. I couldn't look away from his radiant smile as the setting sun behind his head created the most beautiful vision I'd ever seen.

"I love you," he said.

"I love you, too" I replied. "If someone had told me a year ago that my life could someday be this wonderful, this full of beauty and light, I'd have said they were crazy," I said, wrapping my arms around him. "But then I met you, Grayson. And you changed everything."

"Quit being so mushy," he said, nudging me with his elbow and resting his head on my shoulder.

"I'm serious, babe. You know, my dad told me once that life is about how we love. And I always thought I knew what he meant. I thought it meant that we should treat each other well and try to do right by each other. But the way that you love is so much more than that, Grayson. You love me so openly, whole-heartedly, and unconditionally that it takes my breath away. I want to learn to love you like that, even if it takes me the rest of my life."

He looked at me with his beautiful eyes and whispered, "I'm gonna marry you someday."

I kissed him more passionately than I ever had before, knowing without a doubt that everything was as it should be. Just like magic.

Five Years Later | *Adam*

"Tyler Evan King, if you don't get your butt out here we're gonna miss Uncle Scotty's graduation," I called out into the seemingly empty living room.

"Is Aunt Sarah going to be there?" a tiny voice called from the center of the room.

"Yes, buddy, the whole family is going to be there. Uncle Scotty is becoming an official doctor today. It's a big deal," I said, creeping toward the spot where I'd heard his voice.

"Okay, but only if I get to sit with Aunt Sarah and Uncle Drew. *Not* Uncle Mitch and that lady he kisses," he insisted. I finally pinpointed his voice coming from inside the ottoman between the furniture.

"What's wrong with Uncle Mitch and Caroline?" I asked, throwing the lid off of the ottoman to find my son. He laughed and screamed and reached out for me to pick him up.

I lifted his now long and gangly body out and brushed his thick curly hair out of his face. He said, "Uncle Mitch is nice, but that lady always wants to tickle me, and I do *not* like to be tickled."

"You don't like to be tickled, I know. Have you maybe told Caroline that you don't want her to tickle you?" I asked, straightening the tie I'd wrestled onto him a few minutes before.

"No," he said. "She scares me."

"Well, you know Uncle Mitch and Caroline have been together for a long time now. She might be your Aunt Caroline someday just like Uncle Scotty's friend Billy is about to be your Uncle Billy," I said as I put him down and started straightening out my own clothes.

"Yuck," he said. Then a devious smile crossed his face and he tented his fingers together. "Let's destroy her."

"Yeah, let's not do that," I said scooping him back up and heading for the door. "Also, remind me to cut back your TV time — like, a lot."

My family had grown and become a lot closer in the years after Tyler was born. Scotty and Mitch continued to live with me and help me care for Tyler. Drew and Sarah had another daughter, Emma, two years after Abigail. They moved to a city only an hour away from the rest of us when Sarah got a great job offer.

Mitch dated a few girls over the years, no one sticking longer than a few months until Caroline. I hadn't told Tyler yet, but Mitch had recently told me that he and Caroline wanted to move in together. I'd immediately told him that she could move into the house with us. Scotty's fiancé, Billy, whom he had met on the first day of medical school, was also set to move in soon.

Both Scotty and Mitch had started apartment hunting many times over the years, but it never took much to convince them to stay. If we'd had more space, I'm sure we could have talked Drew into moving in too. He and Sarah and the kids spent as much time as possible at our house anyway. It was crowded sometimes, but it was the first time my brothers and I had lived peacefully together, and none of us were in a hurry to give it up. Luckily Billy and Caroline both understood that.

"What about that boy who wants to kiss you, daddy?" Tyler asked as I settled him into his car seat.

"What are you talking about, son?" I asked, feigning ignorance.

"You know, the one who always smiles at you. The one who came to eat turkey the other day? Duh, Daddy," he said, dramatically slapping his hand against his forehead.

"Oh, do you mean Eric?" I asked, bracing myself for whatever he had to say.

"Yes," he said exasperatedly.

"He might be there," I said slyly. Eric and I had reconnected a year before and there was a definite spark there. But the distance was a lot to deal with, and we both had kids to consider. So save for a few visits, we were taking it glacially slow. But his kids were with their mother for Christmas. So he planned to spend the holiday with me. He arrived a couple of weeks early so that he could go with me to Scotty's medical school graduation. I hadn't quite prepared myself to have this conversation with Tyler though. I had been hoping we had more time to see where it was going.

"Well, if he is, you should just kiss him already if you want," Tyler said, squirming in his seat already as I got into the driver's seat.

"You'd be okay with that?" I asked as we pulled away from the house.

"Yes, Daddy," he groaned, dramatically throwing his head back.

"Good to know," I said, grinning at him in the rear view mirror.

As we drove to the university, he told me in detail what he hoped Santa Clause would bring him for Christmas. I tried my best to keep track and memorize anything he'd added since the last time he gave me the list.

I watched proudly as my baby brother graduated again. I felt incredibly lucky to be experiencing that moment standing next to my other brothers just like I had when he'd finished his first degree four years prior and later when Mitch got his business degree.

After the ceremony, we had a huge dinner party back at the house. Eric hadn't made it to the graduation, but he showed up at the party. I tried to keep a respectable distance between us at all times and made sure Tyler was getting most of my attention. After a while, as I sat across from Eric, awkwardly trying to talk over Tyler, Drew came up and grabbed Tyler off of my lap.

"You're killin' me bro," he whispered. "Just jump this guy's bones already. Watching you try to find the most chaste way to flirt is wearing me out. You're a dad, not a priest."

With Tyler no longer between us, Eric scooted his chair closer. We awkwardly laughed and I tried to come up with a new conversation topic. But he made me nervous. Good nervous, butterflies in my stomach nervous, but nervous nonetheless.

Time After Time by Cyndi Lauper came on, a jarring shift from the more modern music that had been playing. I scanned the room and found Drew at the sound system having just changed the song. He made an obscene sexual gesture with his hands, pointed at

Eric, and gave me a thumbs up as he walked away.

"Wasn't this our big prom song?" Eric asked.

"Yeah. My brothers must have found my old yearbooks." I shifted sheepishly in my seat.

"We never did get to dance to this one together," he said, standing in front of me offering his hand. "Shall we?"

I hesitantly took his hand and he led me out into the center of the yard where other couples were dancing. We swayed awkwardly, neither of us sure who should lead, until I finally gave in and let him do it. It was nice. He rested his head on my shoulder and I could smell the sweet shampoo he used wafting in the wind.

"Is the plan really to have Christmas at Mark's?" he asked suddenly.

"Yeah, he has plenty of space. We've been doing a big party for the last few years with our friends and family. It's nice," I explained.

"Isn't that awkward?"

"Not at all. Mitch has been working with him for about five years. They're close friends now. He and

I get along well too. A lot of our friends are mutual, so it just makes sense."

"And you're positive I'm invited?" he pressed.

"Mark's husband Grayson specifically told me to bring you. He's great. They both are. You'll be fine. I promise."

"So he has a husband now? That doesn't make you want to drink?" he asked.

"That, no. Other things do. But I'm not in a hurry to throw away being five years sober," I said. "Besides, I'm really happy for him. Grayson loves him in a way I never could. They're good for each other. I'll find that for myself someday."

He smiled at me and pulled me closer. We kept dancing through a few more songs, getting better at moving together with each one. As we loosened up, I became much less nervous. His laugh was infectious and I found myself acting silly just to make him do it more.

"So, my son thinks we should just kiss already," I said when another slow song started.

"Oh, yeah?" he asked, raising his bushy

eyebrows. "I've always liked that kid." I was just about to lean in to kiss him when Scotty walked up.

"Hey, bubba," he said quietly. "I really appreciate you throwing me this graduation party. But I was hoping you'd be okay if I ducked out."

"What? Where could you possibly have to go that's more important than this?" I asked.

"Billy and I want to go get married," he said, so visibly happy he could only be described as giddy. "We can't wait anymore."

"And you thought you were gonna do this without your brothers? Nuh-uh. Hold on." I went and cut off the music and addressed the crowd. "I'm so sorry everyone, but the party's gonna have to end early. Family emergency."

After everyone but my brothers, their significant others, our children, and Eric had left, I gathered everyone around.

"What's the big emergency?" Mitch asked. "Did you and Eric finally do it?"

"Mitchell," Caroline exclaimed, hitting Mitch's arm and covering Tyler's ears. Tyler rolled his eyes at me as soon as Caroline touched him.

"No," I said curtly, glaring at Mitch. "Our little brother and our new little brother have decided they want to get married. Tonight. So, we have a wedding to throw together."

"No, Adam. You don't have to do anything," Scotty said.

"Task number one goes to Scotty, and it's shut up and go shave that terrible mustache," Sarah said, taking charge. "Kids, go around and find all of the prettiest flowers you can and bring them back here to me. Caroline, you help me make this yard look as nice as possible. Billy, sweetie, you go make sure Scotty looks as presentable as possible. You already look great. Drew, go online and get me ordained so I can marry these crazy kids. The rest of you, clean up the party mess. Let's go people. Move, move, move."

Within an hour, a beautiful wedding was taking place in the backyard. I couldn't help but wish Momma was there to see Scotty get married, but I was sure she was watching somehow. Scotty and Billy asked the kids to stand with them as their best man and co-maids of honor, so Eric and I sat holding hands.

"Maybe that'll be us someday," Eric whispered. "I've kind of had a thing for you for almost 30 years, you know."

"Can you two get a room already?" Drew muttered from behind us.

"Yeah, maybe," I said to Eric. I had no idea what would happen with him. Maybe we would end up together. Maybe we'd go on a few dates and realize it just wasn't meant to be. Either way, I had my family, and that was all I'd ever wanted.

It occurred to me that Scotty and Billy were getting married in almost the same spot where Mark and I had married so long ago. I hoped that their marriage wouldn't turn out the way mine did. But as I looked around at all of the love surrounding me, I knew they could be happy even if it did. After all, I was.

Five Years Later | *Mark*

"Mr. Walker, your family is waiting in the lobby," a voice called from just outside my office at the Refuge.

"Bailey, it's been five years, you can call me Mark," I said, patting him on the back as I walked past him into the lobby. "Although, even after three years of being married to Grayson, I never get tired of the way my heart flutters when somebody calls me Mr. Walker. So maybe stick with that."

Sitting in the waiting area I found Grayson. Dolly was sitting at his feet, and in his lap, our six month old son, Thomas Alexander, "Tommy".

"Hello my beautiful family," I said walking up to greet them. "Oh my goodness, both of my boys look so handsome today." Dolly cried up at me and I scratched her ears. "And of course my favorite girl is looking as beautiful as ever, isn't she?"

"Hi honey," Grayson said, his dazzling smile making my heart race. "You ready?"

"I am always ready to go anywhere with you," I said, taking Tommy from him. "But you're driving because I need to sit in the backseat with this little butterball. I missed him so much."

"But not me, huh?" he asked playfully. "No, it's fine. I get it. I knew my looks would fade eventually. Time to embrace the inevitable circle of life."

"Trust me honey," I said, squeezing his butt as he walked ahead of me toward the car. "You're still sexy as hell. And I'll prove it to you tonight. But first, we have about 20 people coming to the diner for a Christmas dinner that we still need to cook." I turned my attention to Tommy. "Your daddies are what we grownups call "screwed," son. Can you say, 'daddy'?" He gurgled at me incoherently.

When we got back to the diner, Grayson and I alternated between playing with the baby and preparing dinner. On one of my turns to play with Tommy, Grayson caught me staring at him.

"What is it, handsome?" he asked from the kitchen.

"I was just thinking that I love my life with you." I set Tommy down in his playpen and moved into the kitchen and wrapped my arms around Grayson's waist.

"You know, I was just thinking to myself this morning that my life is pretty okay," he said, leaning his head back to kiss my cheek. I slipped my hand under his shirt and up his chest and felt him shiver. "Careful, Mr. Walker. Don't get me all worked up. I have a lot left to do. I don't have time for any of your funny business."

"You sure about that?" I whispered as I kissed his neck and continued to explore his body with my hands. "The baby's preoccupied, most of the work is done, and you are filling out these jeans very nicely."

"Okay, you win," he groaned, turning to face me. I peeled his shirt off of him and started kissing my way down his chest. "But I have to come take this ham out in 15 minutes."

"If it burns, it burns," I whispered, continuing to

kiss his body. And then the baby started crying. "I got it," I sighed, heading back out to pick Tommy up. "Later, I swear."

"I think this officially makes us an old married couple," Grayson called after me as he put his shirt back on.

"There's nobody I'd rather be sex-deprived with babe," I replied.

I settled Tommy down and kept him occupied while Grayson finished cooking. Soon, our many guests started arriving. First came Grayson's parents Donna and Roy. They always arrived earliest and left after everyone else so they could get some time alone with us. I wouldn't have it any other way.

Dr. Rodriguez and Bailey, who had become good friends over the years, and whom I often suspected might have feelings for each other, were next. Kate, who had forgiven me after time passed and provided legal counsel for the Refuge in areas where I couldn't, arrived shortly after them.

Scotty and his new husband Billy were next. It was almost sickening how cute they were together, so clearly in love. Grayson and I had bought them new matching stethoscopes as gifts for their medical school graduation, and they loved them. We knew they would. It was just cheesy enough to fit them.

Amy and Jason then came in with their five children. Shortly after Adam had adopted his son, Amy found out she was pregnant - with triplets. I lost touch with them for a while after the divorce, but it had been easy to pick back up with them after we adopted our own son. Regular trips to the park together had resulted in their invitation to Christmas.

Mitch and his girlfriend Caroline, and Drew and his wife Sarah came next with all of the King children in tow. Drew and Sarah's daughters were the spitting image of their mother, down to her long blonde hair. Adam's son Tyler was as precocious as I would expect any child of Adam's to be. It was strange to see him play with Tommy and realize that in another life, where things between Adam and I worked out, they might have been brothers.

I pushed that thought out of my mind just in time to watch Adam arrive, hand in hand with Eric from his hometown. Mitch had warned me that Grayson had encouraged Adam to bring Eric. I hadn't thought much of it until everyone started asking me if I was okay with it.

I was, unquestionably. I had Grayson and our little family and was happier than I ever thought I could be. I hadn't even had any major OCD symptoms in over a year. My life was good. I wanted the same thing for Adam. So I'd called him a few days prior and reiterated the invitation.

They approached and Adam introduced Eric and me to each other. Eric excused himself to the restroom, leaving Adam and I alone.

"Weird little family we've gathered, huh?" he asked as he began setting out appetizers he'd brought.

"Yeah," I chuckled. "Nice though. It's not what we planned. I mean, I don't think I ever in my wildest dreams could have even begun to plan for... this. But it works."

"It does, doesn't it? Thank you for letting Eric come. I wasn't even positive I wanted to invite him, but the push was nice."

"Of course, Adam. I want you to be happy. Are you?"

"I am," he said, smiling over at Tyler. "What about you?"

I looked over at Grayson, bouncing Tommy on his lap and making silly faces at the other children to make them laugh. I thought back to our wedding day on the beach, and the day he'd asked me to adopt a baby with him. I thought about the day we'd brought Tommy home, and every precious moment since. "I am," I said. "I really am."

Adam grabbed two glasses of water and handed me one. "To happy endings," he said.

"To happy endings," I parroted, tapping my glass against his. I looked back over at Grayson. He and Tommy both smiled up at me and I knew I was already living in mine.

Michael Ryan Webb

ACKNOWLEDGMENTS

My eternal gratitude belongs to my husband, Chance, for being the only one who knew I was writing this book before it was completed, and thus being the only one who had to put up with the many ups and downs throughout the process. He has been the closest thing I've had to an editor and agent, but more importantly, he's been a great partner. This victory belongs to him just as much as it does to me.

Thank you to Darren Cooper, who made sure I survived a dark period and made it out into the light. Everything beautiful in my life I have because he didn't let me give up.

And finally, to my family Cindy, Mady, Mali, Haley, and Nick. Without your love and support over the years, I could not have done this. Thank you.

30096249R00187